# SERIAL POOL ATTENDANT
## SCREENPLAY & TV SERIES BIBLE

*by KARL SMITH*

*orphic house*
* UNITED KINGDOM *

Published by *orphic house*
* UNITED KINGDOM *

# Serial Pool Attendant:

## SCREENPLAY & TV SERIES BIBLE

Published by  orphic house
* UNITED KINGDOM *

Published by Orphic House
95 Longhirst, Middlesbrough TS8 0TD

Creative Director: Karl Peter Smith

© 2010 Karl Peter Smith
First Edition Paperback 2010

**Writers Guild of America, west, Inc.**
SERIAL POOL ATTENDANT
By KARL PETER SMITH - writer
Registration #: 1212062
Effective Date: 07/02/07


**Library of Congress**
United States Copyright Office
101 Independence Avenue SE
Washington, DC 20559-6000
Registration Number: PA 1-607-940
Effective date of registration: August 28, 2008
Performing Arts title: Purge the Soul

**The British Library**
Legal Deposit Office
Boston Spa, Wetherby
West Yorkshire
LS23 7BY
Deposit: August 2010

  Orphic House

        British Library Cataloguing in Publication Data

Smith, Karl Peter.
  Serial pool attendant : screenplay and TV series bible.
  1. Swimming pools--California--Los Angeles--Employees--
  Drama. 2. Murderers--Drama. 3. Television plays--
  Technique.
  I. Title
  822.9'2-dc22


  ISBN-13: 978-0-9566156-1-9

  Also available in HARDBACK
  ISBN-13: 978-0-9566156-7-1

  DOWNLOAD
  www.lulu.com

# Brief script reading refresher...

Location line:
- o **INT.** (interior) or **EXT.** (exterior)
- o Locations are always listed from **LARGER** to **SMALLER**.
- o **DAY** or **NIGHT** (other times like **DAWN** are unnecessary).
- o **DAYDREAM** or **ANCIENT TIMES** can help a reader visualise.

Description:
- o **Describe the environment in the present tense.**
- o **Movement** and **actions** of actors.
- o Possibly a point-of-view **POV** specific to one character.
- o An actor's first appearance is **CAPITALIZED** with a **(micro description)**.

Character name:
- o Always CAPITALIZED when followed by dialogue.
- o Multiple names appearing on the same line means **actors talk together.**

Dialogue:
- o **(parenthicals)** guidelines for the unobvious delivery of dialogue.
- o **(...)** three dots **(ellipsis)** OR **(beat)** a **pause** the length of a drum beat.

FADE IN:

# serial pool attendant
commercial break logo

*DEFENCE AGAINST LIBEL*

*Disclaimer:*

*Serial Pool Attendant* is not a secret expose of any living person; this is purely a work of fiction. References made by any character in this script to real names, persons or events is purely based upon comments or events available and reported widely in the media. Even when events reported in the world media are all considered said and done I still insist this work to be pure fiction.

Unless you're into conspiracies. So zip your mouth shut or there will be consequences.

You still typing this up?

I do not wish to cause any harm to extended family members, we all got family right? That's it you got my story. Enough.

Am I done?

Now get me the hell outta here.

> — The Shark, *High Profile Serial Killer, allegedly.*

EXT.   LOS ANGELES NATIONAL FOREST   FAT CAMP   DAY

BOY SCOUTS erect tents in a clearing.

Deep in the forest fat SCOUT#1 and fat SCOUT#2 swing an axe
at a tree. HENRY (30's) an eloquent wise ass appears in
classic lumberjack outfit holding a crossbow.

> HENRY
> You'd think you boys had just seen the
> boogie man or something. You're
> collecting firewood right? Hand over
> the axe, chop-chop, hold that branch
> steady I'm the biggest "Beaver Ranger"
> round here. Nice badges, we all gotta
> collect something right, gotta belong?
> It's ok, I got my 'big chopper badge'.
> Darn near licensed to tackle anything
> round here.

Branch bends under both Scout's weight.

> HENRY
> Ok, watch them pinkies.

Henry chops and Scout#1's hands catapult into the trees.

Scout#2 runs. A BOLT TWANGS into his back.

> SCOUT#2
> Aargh!

Henry swaggers over to preach...

> HENRY
> Yee, though I walk through the
> Valley of the shadow of death. I
> shall fear no evil, for I am the
> meanest mother fucker in the
> Valley. Not seen Deliverance? So
> much for fat kids watching too much
> TV. Your father will learn from it.
> Tough love. It's a classic!

EXT.   L.A.   SAN CLEMENTE   SUBURBAN GARDEN   DAY

20 YEARS EARLIER . . .

YOUNG HENRY (child) zips up his makeshift N.A.S.A. overall;
a life-of-the-party attention seeker who enjoys getting out
of trouble as much as he likes getting into it. Confident.

YOUNG ALEX (younger sister) tugs at Henry's trouser leg.

MOTHER takes a Polaroid.

> MOTHER
> Cheese.

> ALEX                          HENRY
> Cheese.                       Cheese.

Mother wiggles the developing picture.

> MOTHER
> I'll go show Daddy.


EXT.   NEIGHBOR'S HOUSE   POOL   DAY

A large transparent bowl rests upon Young Henry's head. The
pool's surface ripples before him.

> ALEX (V.O.)
> Life is about exploring the
> unknown, discovery and adventure.
> They wouldn't send a girl to the
> moon if there were any inkling of
> her not coming back now would they?
> What do kids know about mortality
> anyway?

SPLASH - Young Henry sinks like a brick. GLUG of air
bubbles, then silence. Getting to his feet he bounces, every
step, a step on the moon. The tiles shimmer. Above, Young
Alex peers down through the ripples.

> MOTHER (O.S.)
> Alex, Henry? Alex! Henry!

EXT.    POOL    UNDERWATER    DAY

Young Henry's POV - UP TOWARDS THE WATER'S SURFACE

SPLASH -- Young Alex descends into the pool.

OVER THE FENCE

Mother sees the pool surface BUBBLING.


INT.    POOL    UNDERWATER    DAY

Young Alex and Young Henry giggle within the air pocket that
exists in the large hollow bowl.

SPLASH -- FATHER descends into pool.


EXT.    NEIGHBOR'S HOUSE    POOL    DAY

Mother pulls her hair, paces the pool's perimeter.

                    MOTHER
          Oh my god, oh my god.

Young Alex and Young Henry surface, Father holds both by the
scruff of the neck.

                    ALEX (V.O.)
          What was the problem? Henry and I
          got a thick ear for going to the
          moon and back. Our first lunar
          excursion. Space wasn't the scary
          place that everyone had made it out
          to be. We weren't lunatics. Maybe
          if they too had gone to the Sea of
          Tranquility their marriage wouldn't
          have broken up so easily. It was
          all pretty scary. We never saw it
          coming. Still waters run deep, so
          they say.

INT.   DOWNTOWN L.A.    PET SHOP   DAY

ALEX (20's) taps the side of an aquarium. She wears an
assistant's overall. The tank is deep and murky.

                        ALEX
              Here Cujo - here boy!

                        LADY CUSTOMER
              What did you call it?

                        ALEX
              You know, the rabid dog. Duh.

Alex taps her head.

                        ALEX
              Who knows just what's going on
              inside his little head?

She taps the glass.

                        ALEX
              Down boy. Shhh, easy, she's not
              gonna hurt you.

SOON LATER

Two wet legs shake frantically in the air. Alex holds the
Lady customer underwater by the ankles.

                        ALEX
              Shhh, take it easy on her Cujo.

                        ALEX (V.O.)
              I would have been a laughing stock
              if I was known as the 'Serial Pet
              Store Assistant'. The real assistant
              was at lunch and I being the
              opportunist that I am; squeezed in a
              little 'work experience'. Life's one
              big learning curve.

INT.    DOWNTOWN L.A.    THERAPIST OFFICE    DAY

Alex reclines, peers at the textured PLASTER on the ceiling
and compares it to the POSTER of CRATERS ON THE MOON hanging
behind the THERAPIST.

>                    THERAPIST
>           She did have a point; a fish with a
>           dog's name is a weird association.

>                    ALEX
>           But I like fish. Not so keen on
>           dogs, but I do like the film Cujo.

>                    THERAPIST
>           Hmmm.

>                    ALEX
>           Hah, that's clever. The pattern
>           looks just like craters on the moon.

Alex sinks further into the seat and focuses on the ceiling.

>                    THERAPIST
>           Care to share?

>                    ALEX
>           The Sea of Tranquility. I think
>           I've found it. I've found it!
>                (calmer)
>           There are many seas on the moon.
>           Not so many oceans.

Examines fingernails.

>                    ALEX
>           Funny thing, my ex had nice nails.
>           Mine are a lot nicer now. I used to
>           be a nail biter. He used to judge
>           my frame of mind by my nails. If
>           I'd bitten them, I was fucked up.
>           However, I've been eating more
>           carb's, kept myself on the level.
>           Not so many highs or lows. Not too
>           much excitement.

EXT.   WESTLAKE NEIGHBORHOOD   NIGHT

SCREAM from a burning MAN rolling around in flames. Three
PUNKS stands around cajoling him.

Alex cuts through the crowd holding an extinguisher, she
wears an F.D.N.Y. firefighter's uniform.

>                    ALEX
>          Make room, stand aside, coming
>          through!

PUNK#1 crouches, he holds a ZIPPO lighter.

>                    PUNK#1
>          Water boy. Chill. You're too late.

Punk#1 receives a CLUNK in the head with an extinguisher and
falls onto the burning man.

>                    PUNK#1
>          What the fuck!?

>                    ALEX
>          Wrong! I'm just in time.

The flames ignite Punk#1's threads.

>                    PUNK#2
>          You're outta your league little
>          lady.

CLICK of Punk#2's flick-knife.

CRACK of firefighter's pick into Punk#2's skull, his knife
drops to the floor.

O.S. POLICE SIRENS. Alex with bloody-pick searches the
street for an escape route.

>                    ALEX
>                (to Punk#3)
>          You not running?

Punk#3 and Alex make a hasty escape. The extinguisher rolls
and CHUNGS against the curb.

SIRENS

L.A.P.D. Patrol vehicle SCREECHES into the street.

>                    SHARK (V.O.)
>                  (confident, cocky)
>            The vacuum cleaners of crime;
>            L.A.P.D's finest, sucking up all
>            shit no one cares to flush.

O.S. Sound of Shark SUCKING upon a lollipop.

>                    SHARK (V.O.)
>            My name's Shark, I used to be the
>            most notorious serial killer in
>            L.A. Emphasis on the 'used to be',
>            I'm taking a hiatus courtesy of the
>            L.A.P.D. When someone great like
>            myself is off the street, some kid
>            rises to fill the vacuum, its
>            evolution. This is one hell of a
>            true story. Would I lie to you?
>            Trust me, sit back and enjoy the
>            ride. Here I come now, I'm the
>            handsome one.

EXT.   L.A.   HUNTINGTON BEACH   DAY

"THE SHARK" stylized graffiti, written upon a surfboard
stuck in the sand. SHARK (late 20's) sucks a lollipop and
sunbathes on a towel; tips his sunglasses in the direction
of a passing babe.

VICTORIA (30's) jogs in lavender bikini, spinsterish with
integrity; confident and business-like she dots the I's and
crosses the T's leaving all competition in her wake.

                    SHARK
          The strongest wave can break a
          woman's back. That is, if you let
          it get right on top of you. Have
          you ever been bent over by a beast
          so huge it makes your spine pop?

She giggles.

                    SHARK
          That's what I'm talking about,
          laughter in the face of adversity.

Motions to Adonis-like BODYBUILDERS pumping weights in the
shallows.

                    SHARK
          Watch out for the predators in the
          shallows.
               (mumbles)
          They're more likely to bite each
          other in the ass than catch a wave.

Runs hand through hair. Springs to feet in one motion and
grabs surfboard.

                    SHARK
          If I'm not back to drive you all
          the way home just leave your number
          in the sand.

Jogs to the surf.

EXT.    HUNTINGTON BEACH    PIER BEACH SHOP    CAR PARK    DAY

Shark exits the beach with his board under arm and laughs at
a note poking out of his sunglasses case.

Alex loiters beside a yellow Volkswagen Beetle

                    ALEX
               Shark?

Shark walks by.

                    ALEX
               Shark? The serial Shark.

                    SHARK
               Look kid. You must have me mixed up
               with some other handsome dude.
               Unlucky. Best of luck in your hunt
               for this Shark dude.

                    ALEX
               I know it's you.

Alex rolls up the arm of her blouse to reveal a tattoo of
Shark, a portrait of the very man stood before her.

                    SHARK
               What are you? Some sick kind of a
               wannabie?

                    ALEX
               This your car?

                    SHARK
               Do I look like Al Bundy? Mine is
               the Cadillac 'round the corner.
               Ease up on the heat kid; look fresh
               here comes the babe that owns the
               thing. Stay schtum, just smile.

Victoria approaches the Beetle.

EXT.    CADILLAC (MOVING)    DAY

Shark drives, Alex passenger.

>                    SHARK
>           Paroled for good behavior would you
>           believe it? Role model prisoner. I
>           had my solicitor rearrange a
>           magazine exclusive for my release,
>           model citizen; very... Hollywood,
>           will keep my face in the media for
>           a while. Even got a three-picture
>           deal for my life story. Want a good
>           solicitor? I'll refer you.

Shakes an electronic tag on his ankle. Checks watch.

>                    SHARK
>           The price of freedom. If I'm off
>           the beach by sundown, I'm not
>           violating my parole.

Gives Alex the once over.

>                    SHARK
>           You're not saying much kid.

>                    ALEX
>           My name's Alex.

>                    SHARK
>           Yeah Alex, you said, so where you
>           wanna be?


PULLS UP OUTSIDE SWIMMING BATHS

Alex exits the Cadillac.

>           Shark                    ALEX
>     They used to call me--    --The Shark. Yeah I know.

>                    SHARK
>           So you're my biggest fan hey? Stick
>           around kid you might learn
>           something.

EXT.    L.A.    HUNTINGTON BEACH    DAY

Shark catches some rays; a silhouette falls upon his body.

> SHARK
> Is someone drowning? You had better
> have a good reason for blocking a
> man's Sun.

> ALEX
> It's me, Alex

He leaps up and slaps her fondly on the shoulder.

> SHARK
> Been thinking about you. Alex, yes.
> My Padowan. Shoot much pool Alex?

Wiggles fingers.

> SHARK
> Good for the pinkies.

They walk off together, Alex under Shark's wing.

> SHARK
> Back in the days when killers were
> proper bad asses. On the run. All
> avoiding the law. None of this
> Columbine killing spree shit then
> kill yourself fad. I mean where's
> that get you? Where's the legacy?
> What's left to nurture? You my
> friend are a protégée. About to
> learn from a master of death -- and
> every Zorro must have his secret
> cave.

INT.    SAN DIEGO COUNTY    OCEANSIDE SAFE HOUSE    NIGHT

Shark wears a welder's mask on his forehead. An insane
driven look upon his face as he pulls at the mask. SPARKS
fly from the meat cleaver pushed against a grind-stone.

> SHARK
> Ever see the Sorcerer's apprentice?
> Some crazy shit animation about --
> well, I don't know what it's about.
> I thought I knew what it was about.
> But, anyway -- back in the days of
> stop motion animation Walt must
> have been keeping the good shit for
> himself. Dumptee-dumptee dump de-
> dumpadee dumptee-dumptee dump.

Alex tops up Shark's glass of lemonade.

> SHARK
> Is it just me or can you see
> dancing elephants?

> ALEX
> It's only lemonade, not Champagne.
> That's what you meant by good shit
> yeah?

> SHARK
> Just lemonade kid? Sure, those
> bubbles go right to the brain.
> You'll have to give me granny's
> recipe.

Squints. Takes a swig.

> SHARK
> Hair of the dog.

Chops through a watermelon with one cleave.

> SHARK
> Oh, yes. Now we're cooking.

INT.    UCLA CAMPUS    CINEMA    DAY

Dark room. CLICK of PROJECTOR casting images of a BASEBALL
stadium over the heads of STUDENTS onto a big SCREEN.

Victoria, shady, book in hand stands behind a lectern.

                         VICTORIA
                    Lights please.


CLOSE ON: "1001 MOVIES YOU MUST SEE BEFORE YOU DIE".

French polished NAILS tap upon the TOME'S SPINE.

BACK TO SCENE

                         VICTORIA
                    The Bible.
                         (beat)
                    Everything you'll ever need to know
                    to pass this course.
                         (beat)
                    Beg, steal or borrow. I've even
                    known people to kill just to own
                    one. A little joke of mine.

O.S. RIPPLE of laughter. Victoria opens on page 12.

                         VICTORIA
                    An 'aye' to 'zee' of possibilities.
                    Given the almost impossible task
                    ahead, choose wisely. Creativity is
                    the sign of a complex mind. How is
                    the killer to escape? (beat) Any
                    quick witted Spartans willing to
                    face-off?

Alex in silhouette raises a hand. Victoria squints and
points.

                         VICTORIA
                    Yes, impress me; be as creative as
                    you can.

INT.    OCEANSIDE SAFE HOUSE    KITCHEN    DAY

CLOSE ON: Henry's hands CHOPPING an ONION into fine
slithers.

HENRY
(sing)

'Cause I'm a man of many wishes.
Hope my premonition misses. What I
really need. My eyes are open wide
and they always start to cry.

BACK TO SCENE

Henry wears SWIMMING TRUNKS and GOGGLES.

O.S. DING DONG

HENRY

It's open!

Enter Victoria with a BOTTLE OF WINE.

HENRY

The swimming goggles create a
barrier between the oil and the
tear ducts preventing any stinging.

Victoria raises the BOTTLE.

VICTORIA

Is that right?
(beat)
And the trunks?

HENRY

Morals. You wouldn't expect me to
do this naked now would you?
(beat)
Glasses are in the cabinet. Oh and
by the way, I don't think she
suspects a thing.

INT.    UCLA CAMPUS    CINEMA    DAY

Alex waits with a SCREENPLAY in hand. Victoria hands over
the paperback 'YOUR SCREENPLAY SUCKS'.

>                    VICTORIA
>          This may help with a few tricky
>          spots in your last submission. If
>          your protagonist doesn't survive,
>          in the end, the whole thing flops.

They swap.

>                    VICTORIA
>          This your 'Houdini' escape? So you
>          think you can get away with a
>          murder in front of a thirty-six
>          thousand strong crowd?

>                    ALEX
>          Trust me, it's a killer script.

She walks away.

Victoria holds a script entitled 'Murder in The Fourth'.

>                    VICTORIA
>          Murder in the fourth. Hmmm.


INT.    SAN DIEGO COUNTY    OCEANSIDE SAFE HOUSE    DAY

Alex searches a tool rack. Silhouettes exist of missing
items -- scythe, chainsaw, sword and shears. Only a hacksaw
remains.

O.S. Victim moaning.

Alex peers through Victim's wallet.

>                    ALEX
>          None descript. Bit of cash.
>          Perfect.

A male VICTIM lay face-up with his head in a metal vice.

                    ALEX
          No one's going to miss you.

Turns the vice tighter. Victim SCREAMS.

                    ALEX
          Jesus Christ, I've got neighbors.

Flexes Hacksaw. SHIZA-MOLAR logo shines in his face.

                    ALEX
          Say cheese.

Louder gurgling SCREAM.

Alex's arm moves back and forth in a jerky motion.

O.S. CHOKING GURGLING COUGHING

Specks of blood pepper Alex's face.

                    ALEX
          Jesus what a bleeder. Did you know
          Shiza-molar is German for shitty
          teeth? Ironic eh?


INT.    HARDWARE STORE    DAY

Alex stands at a rack of hacksaws, pen behind ear.

The Proprietor comes from the back room with a new Schiza-
molar hacksaw in its protective cardboard sheath.

                    PROPRIETOR
          That's the third this month, are
          you eating them?

                    ALEX
          Someone must be.

                    PROPRIETOR
          Blade chip?

                    ALEX
          You should have a word with that
          Schiza-molar manufacturer, that's a
          bit of a mouthful.

                    PROPRIETOR
          Sign here - and here.

Alex signs document with her own pen.

                    ALEX
          How much postage, you're killing
          me.
                    (with receipt)
          I must be keeping you in business.

                    PROPRIETOR
          Service with a smile.


INT.    DOWNTOWN NEW YORK    SHRINK'S OFFICE    DAY

Shrink picks up a blunt pencil and begins to sharpen it.

                    SHRINK
          So Alex, what mythological creature
          is on your mind today?

                    ALEX
          Ha ha very funny. Spiders actually,
          I have spiders on my mind.

                    SHRINK
          You have a fear of spiders?

                    ALEX
          No. I was thinking of the Trapdoor
          spider. Heard of it?

                    SHRINK
          They live in a hole with a lid and
          pop out to catch passing prey?

                    ALEX
          That's them.

>               SHRINK
> You may fear being caught by an
> unseen force.

>               ALEX
> Nah not that, I was worried for the
> spiders, thinking whether they
> suffered from agoraphobia; if they
> had a fear of going out?

Shrink's pencil snaps in his hand.


EXT.   DOWNTOWN NEW YORK   DAY

Below the NEW YORK skyline.

SHOP WINDOW: A TV set plays the STOCK footage of John
Travolta on the sidewalk swinging a tin of paint.

Alex mirrors by swinging an EXTREME SPORTS bag. She can't
help but smell the perfume of a passing lady… Enter Victoria
who dips the wide brim of her hat to avoid recognition.

>               ALEX
>     Lavender?

Billboard: 'BLUE ICE' beer. A HUNKY BLACKSMITH with broad
smile quenches a red-hot poker into a vat of WATER.

Alex walks the sidewalk to the Bee Gees "Staying Alive".

Passing VAN emblazoned with 'BLUE ICE THE REFRESHING BRAND'.

>               ALEX (V.O.)
> The <u>Big Apple</u>; where all the little
> apples grow up. Makes me feel a
> little Nemo-ish.
>         (shakespearean accent)
> I am but a fish in a school of
> plankton; waiting to be eaten by a
> basking shark.

NEWSPAPER STAND - Takings NEWS from VENDOR Alex motions to
the vendor's 'Blue-ice' wristband.

                    ALEX
          Is that the latest trend?

                    VENDOR
          A collectible. One hundred ring
          pulls. It's 'Blue ice'.

                    ALEX
          Collectible?

                    VENDOR
                (motions to billboard)
          'Black ice' now that takes one
          thousand. People would kill for
          that shit.

                    ALEX
          You're kidding me?

Vendor spots Alex's F.D.N.Y. lapel.

                    VENDOR
          On duty right? Well, save those
          ring pulls for me.

RATTLES a half-full bucket of ring-pulls.

                    VENDOR
          Stay fresh babe.

A ZIPPO lighter lands in the Vendor's bucket.

                    ALEX
          Don't get burnt.

                    VENDOR
          God bless you. Have a nice day.

INT.   24 HOUR STORE    NIGHT

Alex, stocking on head, holds a meat cleaver. The PROPRIETOR
pulls cash bills from the till.

                    ALEX (V.O.)
          Collectibles give a person a sense
          of purpose. A goal to strive for.
          Stamp collecting is advisable; so
          says my shrink, but I don't find it
          half as enjoyable, as say robbery.
          The stockings are French, 15
          denier, regular nylon, with a
          gossamer sheen belonging to only
          ultra sheer stockings. Available
          from any good high street store.

The Proprietor wears a gold watch and 'Blue-ice' wristband.

                    ALEX
          Your fuckin' wrist! Take it off!

                    ALEX (V.O.)
          And -- they don't easily ladder.

                    PROPRIETOR
          Ok, ok.

He removes his gold watch and puts it on the counter.

                    ALEX
          The fuckin' band. The fuckin
          wristband!

                    PROPRIETOR
          Hey? What?

He nervously removes the wristband which Alex snatches.

                    PROPRIETOR
          Ok ok.

The Proprietor picks up the cash from the till and holds it
out.

Walks away.

> ALEX
> If you phone the cops I'll fucking
> torch the place!

LATER

FLASHING LIGHTS, a Fire Appliance illuminates the front of
the Store. The CREW douses flames that lick the outside of
the building.

Alex watches from a car in the distance. Calm Opera music
plays upon the radio.

> ALEX
> What kind of sicko torches a
> convenience store; what a
> neighborhood.

EXT.   CAR (MOVING)   NIGHT

A BAG LADY (60) pushes a trolley full of cans across the
street.

Alex slows at the crossroads. A Blue-ice band circles her
wrist. A stocking lay on the passenger seat.

> ALEX (V.O.)
> Some people. They'll collect any
> shit to feel a part of society.

She leans forwards on the dash.

> ALEX
> That's gotta be a bum job.

INT.    SWIMMING BATHS    NIGHT

Alex mops the poolside. Ceiling lights flicker with the
MANAGER at the switch.

>                    ALEX
>         Sir?

>                    MANAGER
>         Filter, lights and locks, don't
>         forget them, and in that order
>         Alex. Check the filter; body-hair
>         clumps. We have elementary phys-ed
>         in the morning. Make sure this
>         place is clean.

>                    ALEX
>         Crystal.


INT.    SWIMMING BATHS    DAY, DAYDREAM

SQUEAKY sound of a mop upon tiles. Alex hurriedly mops up a
scene of utter carnage. Blood covers most pool equipment,
diving board, pools inflatables etc.


EXT.    ELEMENTARY SCHOOL BUS    SWIMMING BATHS    DAY

A TEACHER leaps off the bus.

>                    TEACHER
>         I'll just confirm the booking.
>         Everybody wait in an orderly
>         fashion.

Teacher walks to the entrance.

With his hand on the door handle, the growing sound of the
rowdy bus behind diverts his attention for a second; he
huffs, turns and walks back towards the bus.

INT.    SWIMMING BATHS    DAY, DAYDREAM

Alex just seems to be smearing blood around with a mop
sodden with blood. She removes her lifeguard shirt
scrunching it like a rag and runs to entrance with a SQUEAKY
slipper sound to wipe away blood on and around door handle.


EXT.    SWIMMING BATHS    ELEMENTARY SCHOOL BUS    DAY

CHILDREN SCREAM. Teacher enters the bus.

                    TEACHER
          Right! Hold it. Everyone. Everyone!
          Simmer down, or I'll give you
          something to scream about.

The noise subsides.

                    TEACHER
          Ok. Everybody? Ready to swim?

                    CHILDREN
          YEAH!

All disembark and follow Teacher.


INT.    SWIMMING BATHS    DAY, DAYDREAM

A decapitated head peers over the rim of a bloody bucket.
Alex slides like a Curler across the floor pushing the
bucket along with a towel. She lets go and the bucket slides
and slams into a pile of other macabre buckets; arms and
legs hang out of each. She stands, chest out. The head now
looks back over the rim. Alex with hand on heart.

                    ALEX
          Yes! And the gold goes to Alex Lake
          of the "U" "S" of "A". Once pool
          attendant now Curling champion of
          the free world.

Silhouettes of Children appear on the other side of the
entrance's partition.

The door handle turns.

>           ALEX
> Outside the area, with no time on
> the clock, three point shot.

A bloody lifeguard shirt spins high into the air and lands
upon the head in the bucket. Alex punches the air.

>           ALEX
> The crowd go wild. GOLD!


INT.    SWIMMING BATHS    DAY

SCREAMING Children. Alex wakes in her lifeguard armchair.

>           ALEX
> Yes, the crowd really are going
> wild.

Alex blows her whistle.

>           ALEX
> Hey, rules! No running.

LATER

Alex in lifeguard seat. BUZZ from tannoy. Blows whistle.

>           ALEX
> Everybody out the water!

Waves the children to the shallows.

>           ALEX
> Hurry or I'll release the sharks.

A CHILD in the pool turns around to see a shark's fin. The
child's eyes pop out. An inflatable shark bobs to the
surface.

                    ALEX
                (mimicking JAWS)
            It's just a school of Blue fins.

The Child goes hysterical.

                    ALEX
            Jaws? Spielberg? Spiel who? Get
            outta here.

Alex takes a mop and reaches into the pool. The Child grabs
the end and swims to the side.

                    TEACHER
            I think that little outburst may
            jeopardize your position in this
            establishment.

                    ALEX
                (jokingly)
            What?
                (seriously)
            My job?

The Teacher turns.

Alex raises the mop above the Teacher's head and breaths
deeply.

THUD.

INT.    SWIMMING BATHS    CUBICLES    DAY

A beach towel partially hides a bloody CHAINSAW in Alex's
hand.

                    ALEX
          Ties on, buttons all done up?

Children appear all-smart except for the first BOY who has
his top button undone.

                    ALEX
          What did I say about buttons?

Chainsaw PURRS into action. Alex kisses it.

                    ALEX
          Who's game for catchy kisses?

All Children SCREAM.


EXT.    SWIMMING BATHS    ELEMENTARY SCHOOL BUS    DAY

The DRIVER looks to the building. Silhouettes get to the
door but buckets of blood slosh upon the glass to the WHINE
of a chainsaw.

                    ALEX (O.S.)
          Own up, who pissed in my pool?

Distant SCREAMS fade away.

INT.   UCLA CAMPUS   CINEMA   DAY

Victoria holds the screenplay "Murder in the fourth".

                    VICTORIA
          We have amongst us a gifted
          student. I would like to read a
          passage from her latest submission,
          one that talks about action,
          emotion… balance.
                  (reading)
          A lunatic's trigger originates deep
          in the subconscious mind. Some past
          event; more likely, several events.
          As a child -- a grazed knee -- a
          hug, a kiss off momma, everything
          seems all better, you feel great.
          Then you bleed, you receive love.
          It doesn't take much too associate
          blood with love; a familiar feeling
          of excitement. Yet here, water
          keeps me calm. When the shit hits
          the fan, I am as cool as cucumber.
          But violence -- too much and it
          takes flowing water to bring me
          down. Twisted logic. Yin and Yang.
          I must maintain the balance.

INT.   OPERA HOUSE   NIGHT

Alex and Shark have a birds-eye view of the stage. An OPERA
SINGER walks the boards.

Shark raises his hand; 3-D glasses are taped to a candy-
floss stick.

                    SHARK
          If only I could share my incite, my
          knowledge, you could see life's
          true colors just the way I do.

He lowers his glasses, looks to the ceiling at the rear of
the theatre, and exits the rear curtain leaving Alex alone.

CLOSE ON: SPOTLIGHT, a blue filter drops in front; a red
filter drops down in front of a second.

BACK TO SCENE

Below, the Opera singer bathes in red and blue light.
Shark retakes his seat.

                    ALEX
          Sweet.

MUSIC: Adagio for strings (Extract) (Barber) From PLATOON.

                    ALEX (V.O.)
          Opera changes everyone's
          perspective of music. We all have
          experiences, ones we take for
          granted. (beat) The baton sways,
          orchestrating the tears in my eyes,
          tugging my heart strings. I cannot
          stop my eyes from stinging. I am
          powerless; dominated by the music,
          I fall, submissively, for a moment,
          weak, powerless, but in a sense
          free.

Her eyes sparkle with tears.

INT.    RECORD STORE    DAY

DJ (20's) plays a retro collection of 'Heavy Metal'.

A heavily pierced CUSTOMER in black waits patiently.

> DJ
> With a hidden message from Satan if
> played backwards.

> CUSTOMER
> I was actually looking for a Stevie
> Nicks album.

> DJ
> The rare hologram single 'Rooms on
> Fire'?

> CUSTOMER
> The latest release.

> DJ
> Regular? We don't do regular. This
> isn't fast food I do here. Get out
> my shop you freak, I'm insulted.

TINKLE of door chime, enter Alex in 'LIFEGUARD' T-shirt.

Customer shoulder barges Alex on his way out.

> ALEX
> Some people.

> CUSTOMER
> Alex my good friend.

Alex flashes her 'Pool' badge.

> DJ
> New job? Stop scaring my customers,
> here a second.

> ALEX
> You're going great guns doing that
> with your 'Thrasher Death Metal'
> promo.

                    DJ
          It's an acquired taste.

                    ALEX
          Yes, I must broaden my narrow taste
          in the classics.

DJ lifts a book from under the counter and holds it as a
waiter would present a bottle of wine.

                    DJ
          Not in the same ball park as
          Handel's Water Music but this may
          be something to satisfy your
          weirdness. I have to keep my
          reputation of pleasing my most
          loyal freaks.

Takes out CD which acts as a bookmark.

                    DJ
          No non-descript brown wrap in this
          quality establishment; it's not a
          porn shop. (beat) The Marquis de
          Sade's first work.

Alex smiles.

                    DJ
          There's a place in 'Extreme
          Thrasher-Metal Heaven' for you, you
          know that don't you?

                    ALEX AS ROD SERLING
          Picture a world. If a dog sees in
          black and white does a bat dream in
          sound?

                    DJ
          Page 47. The Marquis has a meat
          sandwich with his gardener and
          house servant. A tasty novel.

TINKLE of entrance chime. Bag-lady enters.

                    DJ
          Loads of man-fat.

                    ALEX
          Gross. But put it on the tab.

                    BAG LADY
          You youngsters should eat more
          healthily; you should try the
          'George Foreman Grill'.

DJ and Alex share a chuckle.

                    BAG LADY
          I am looking for Sinatra.

Alex steps back, waves the book, and exits the store.

                    DJ
               (whispers to lady)
          My father is a great -- huge --
          Sinatra fan. Picture discs,
          rarities, a collector's paradise.
          If it aint available I may have it
          in my rare bootleg collection.

Holds up an audio cassette.

                    DJ
          One and only copy. Only the man
          himself, singing in the bath.

                    BAG LADY
          No Beta-max sonny, got it on Blue-
          ray?

DJ juggles a CD from beneath the counter.

                    BAG LADY
          That'll do. Take Plastic?

                              DJ
             Sure, you have a mailing address?

                           BAG LADY
             Don't you want my email?

Bag-lady removes prosthetic mask and beneath is Victoria.

                     VICTORIA AS BAG LADY
             How is she?

                              DJ
             Not exactly a wistful woman of the
             world. Want me to get her a pistol?

                           VICTORIA
             A sword makes a warrior--

                              DJ
             --as much as a feather in your hair
             makes you an Eagle. Yeah was
             thinking that myself.

                           VICTORIA
             Anyway she hates guns; prefers
             knives, blades. It's a self harm
             thing.


**DJ rubs his chin and looks to the CLASSIC MOVIE SECTION
where hangs a poster of Kurosawa's 'The Seven Samurai'.**


INT.   CINEMA   DAY

Darkness. Alex and Shark's face flicker in a strobe light.
Both wear 3-D glasses. No one else in the cinema wears them.

They mirror each other; eating from a large carton of
popcorn.

SOUND of Hitchcock's classic shower scene from 'Psycho'.

A female usher walks the aisle.

                    SHARK
          Hey, does this Motel sell cola? A
          man could die of thirst in here.


EXT.   CINEMA   DAY

FAMILIES queue for either 'Psycho' or 'Free Willy 2'. Alex
holds her 3-D glasses and squints in the light of day. Shark
wears his 3-D's the same way he would sunglasses.

                    SHARK
          It's all in the mind. You just
          never see the knife strike her,
          these just add a bit of color to
          the good old black and white. Ever
          see 'Vertigo'?

Moves hand back and forth, in and out. Some fathers
jump from the 'Free Willy' queue to the 'Psycho' queue

                    SHARK
          That zoomy thing they do with the
          lens; all good stuff. This reminds
          me; remind me to check my genealogy
          tree to see if we're related.

                    ALEX
          Just what are we doing here?

                    SHARK
          Don't question it girl. It's all
          character building.

INT.   METROPOLITAN MUSEUM   GALLERY OF GREAT MASTERS   DAY

Portrait of WHISTLER'S MUM; Shark and Alex sit with ice
creams.

                    SHARK
           Life imitates art. Art imitates
           life. However, whoever wishes for a
           mother like that or a wife needs
           their heads checking.

Alex looks bemused.

                    SHARK
           Like fashion, either set the trend
           or follow it.

                    GUARD
           Excuse me, no eating in the gallery.

                    SHARK
           A certain Motel proprietor would
           have given her a good stuffing.
               (realizing his words)
           Oh, but not in that way.

Shark stands and licks his ice cream in the Guard's face.

                    SHARK
           Come my protégée, we are not
           welcome here.

Alex gives her ice cream a lick. The Guard gives a mean face
and Alex flinches, jumping to Shark's side.

NEXT GALLERY

A CURATOR addresses a crowd of TOURISTS. A **T-REX** skeleton
dominates the room. Shark and Alex try to blend in.

The pursuing Guard scans the crowd.

Shark beats the Curator to a microphone.

>                    SHARK
>           The ultimate killing machine with
>           the ability to give one nasty
>           hickey. That is if he could catch
>           you. We monkeys with opposing
>           thumbs and brains bigger than a
>           walnut just outsmarted the big
>           plucked chicken.
>                    (MORE)

One TOURIST wearing an ELVIS T-SHIRT catches Shark's eye.

>                    SHARK CONT'D
>           Rex was King of the Dinosaurs. The
>           Elvis of prehistory, until he
>           decided to leave the building, and
>           ultimately the planet.
>                    (to Elvis fan)
>           See what I did there?
>                    (to Guard)
>           Catch.

Shark catapults the microphone through the air.


INT.   METROPOLITAN MUSEUM   ENTRANCE   DAY

The Guard watches them leave.

BEHIND HIS BACK:   A 'Venus de Milo' statue in the foyer sports
two ice cream cones for breasts.


INT.   SAN DIEGO COUNTY   OCEANSIDE SAFE HOUSE   DAY

Alex runs a finger along the spines of an extensive DVD
library. 'HOOK' PETER PAN is out of place. INSIDE IS A
FOLDED NOTE, on the outside "To die would be an awfully big
adventure" signed with Victoria's signature LIPSTICK KISS.

Unfolding note.

VICTORIA (V.O.)
Your target is the captain of a
Polo team. The reason being
disseminated on a need to know
basis and all you need to know is
how to play Polo. Can you ride?

ALEX (V.O.)
A subtle hook -- and about as
subtle a hook as they come.  An
adventure led by a boy who can
clearly fly by the seat of his
pants and I obviously cannot. I
guess I am going to have to go
about this the hard way.


INT.    EXTREME SPORT SHOP    DAY

Beneath a POSTER of the Swiss EIGER. Alex squints at the
goofy looking SALES CLERK.

ALEX
Would that rope hold a three-man
crew on the north face of the
Eiger?

SALES CLERK
High tensile. Would hold a baby
Elephant.

ALEX
Excellent. You know your stuff. I'm
actually after a Polo Mallet.

SALES CLERK
Cash or plastic?

INT.   EXTREME SPORT SHOP   DAY, DAYDREAM

Hits Sales clerk in the face with the mallet.

BACK TO SCENE

Alex with a wallet full of hundred dollar bills.

> ALEX
> Take Benjamin Franklin?


INT.   SAN DIEGO COUNTY   OCEANSIDE SAFE HOUSE   NIGHT

Shark drills a new hole in the head of the Polo mallet and blows the sawdust from it, then peers through the hole.

> ALEX (O.S.)
> And the point of that was?

Shark picks up a white cane and slides it into the new hole; it SQUEAKS in tightly.

> SHARK
> Like a glove.

Grasps the leather grip and swings it.

> SHARK
> HA HAH!
> (calmly)
> Shhh, tomorrow, it's a surprise.

EXT.   POLO FIELD   DAY

Mounted PLAYERS group at either end of the field.

Alex dresses in tight jockey silks. Shark double checks the
mallet is secure.

                    ALEX
          I look ridiculous.

                    SHARK
          Right, the game plan. You have to
          be in it to win it.

Shark slaps her shoulder.

                    SHARK
          You're sub'. A crash-course never
          hurt anyone. You'll soon feel your
          way 'round.

                    ALEX
          Like this? This isn't a Paris
          catwalk. It's a man's game, I'm a
          girl. And I can't ride. Just what
          do ya expect me to do?

A SPECTATOR leans in on their conversation. Shark coughs.

                    SHARK
          Score a goal, conversion, whatever
          they call it. Punt ermmm that way
          towards that end. Ride like a
          Valkyrie.

Leans forward, delivers a warm hug.

                    SHARK
               (whispers)
          I'll be in the car park.

LATER

HORSEMEN face-off.

Alex sits high in the saddle.

The REFEREE blows hard on the starting WHISTLE.

Distant MUSIC blasts from the car park. Shark's car is aligned parallel with the pitch. The engine ticks over. WAGNER'S 'The Ride Of The Valkyries' gets louder.

All HORSES gallop to the center spot.

Shark's car travels parallel with the galloping horses.

Earsplitting volume 'The Ride Of The Valkyries'.

Alex swings the mallet at the ball on the center spot, the cane's sheath flies away to reveal a sword. She looks to Shark, all teeth and drunk with music.

Alex swings decapitating the opposing Captain.

Shark skids off the grass CACKLING with laughter. Burns rubber in the car park and he's off!

Alex on horseback gallops into the car park and after the vanishing Cadillac.

INT.   SAN DIEGO COUNTY   OCEANSIDE SAFE HOUSE   NIGHT

Alex paces the room with renewed enthusiasm. Shark bites the
cherry from the umbrella in his cocktail glass.

                    ALEX
          That was you? I remember that
          article , 'Murders In The Fall'?

                    SHARK
          Yup. I had it covered from all
          angles -- so I thought.


INT.   BEAUTY PARLOR   DAY, MEMORY

Shark reclines to soft music, he receives a manicure. The
BEAUTY THERAPIST moves to the till and he palms her nail
file.

                    SHARK (V.O.)
          The prices they charge for doing
          fingers, I figured I'd bought the
          tools for the job.

BACK TO SAFE HOUSE

Shark files off his fingerprints; buffs them smooth.


EXT.   ALLEY   DAY, MEMORY

Shark hands a HOBO a few dollars for his boots. All other
HOBOS in the vicinity pull off their boots and wave them in
his direction. Shark waves them away.

                    SHARK (V.O.)
          That was my footprints solved. Do I
          look like a gimpy-legged hobo? No.
          Later, Cinderella here will be
          shitting pumpkins when the boots
          fit snugger than O.J's glove.

EXT.    VICTIM'S HOUSE    NIGHT, MEMORY

Snow covers the ground. Shark peers through the window.

> SHARK (V.O.)
> The media called it 'Murders in the
> Fall'. Trust me it was Winter, but
> that's not such a snappy headline.

HUSBAND and WIFE argue... She receives a slap.

> SHARK (V.O.)
> I was only out for kicks but I just
> didn't like the way that guy was
> pushing her around.

Shark dons his latex gloves.

> ALEX (V.O.)
> Why gloves?

> SHARK (V.O.)
> They can get your prints off
> anything these days, even gloves. I
> told you I was covering all angles.

> ALEX (V.O.)
> So how'd they catch you?

LATER

Shark takes a piss next to the kitchen window.

> SHARK (V.O.)
> In autumn I was fine. Winter was an
> even bigger fall! Would you
> believe, they got me by my DNA,
> from a piss-hole in the snow?

INT.   SAN DIEGO COUNTY   OCEANSIDE SAFE HOUSE   NIGHT

Shark and Alex relax.

> SHARK
> I took the 'plea bargain' under the
> condition they didn't call me the
> 'piss hole peeping-tom'. I even made
> up some violent shit and did extra
> time. A few extra years were fine;
> three square meals and the nickname
> 'Shark' was worth every word of
> bullshit from my purdy lips.

> ALEX
> So you didn't kill fifty-seven nuns
> and a troop of eunuchs?

> SHARK
> I hate to break it to you. I'm a
> pathological liar. I'll confess to
> any shit for a bit of notoriety.
> The H-bomb for instance was my
> idea, I only patented 'Aye' to 'Gee',
> the CIA just took it one-step
> further than I intended. It was I
> that melted the ice-caps and
> punctured the ozone layer. Heard
> Mohammed Ali's recent poetry? Not
> really, that's a stutter I gave him
> with a single punch. In the blue
> corner, 'the Shark'. Yeah, he never
> saw that one coming either.

Shark squeezes beer can, struggles, stamps on it instead.

> ALEX
> But you make such wonderful killing
> tools. You didn't fake them! I
> don't care if the stories aren't
> real. It's quite funny bravado.

> SHARK
> Bravado, you think? Did I mention
> Halloween? That's a tastey tale.

EXT.   VICTIM'S HOUSE   DAY

Children 'Trick Or Treat' in 'Wizard of Oz' costumes. The
LION, TIN MAN and SCARECROW; their mother is DOROTHY.

The Lion rings the bell. Shark answers in a Freddy costume
with knives for fingers.

> SHARK
> I am your worst nightmare. Come
> inside. See if you can pass the
> Wizard's trial of - of - OZ! Hehe.


INT.   VICTIM'S HOUSE   LIVING ROOM   NIGHT

Halloween decorations, Pumpkins, Cobwebs etc. The Lion, Tin
man, scarecrow and Dorothy stand in front of four Black
boxes; each with a slit on the top.

> SHARK
> I lay before you Egyptian canopic
> jars. Everyone seen 'The Mummy?'
> Well those boxes; available in any
> good high street store; only
> cheaper, contain the body organs of
> the dead from 'Little Creek
> Cemetery'. Who's first? The brave
> Lion eh, that's fitting, I hope you
> like snakes. Dig deep, get the
> treat from inside. Go on. You're
> first.

The Lion's bare hand slides inside; he squirms, and then
pulls out a chocolate bar and laughs at the wet spaghetti
covering it.

> SHARK
> Tin man, you must reach inside the
> dead man's chest.

Tin man reaches inside box number two, squirms, and pulls
out a packet of crisps covered in jelly.

                    SHARK
          Scaredy-cat Scarecrow next. This
          box contains dead men's eyeballs.
          Get your treat. You'll need both
          hands for this.

Scarecrow puts both hands in the box. Flinches and squirms,
then pulls out a handful of hard-boiled eggs and a packet of
party poppers.

                    SHARK
          Too easy, hold on hold on.

Shark puts a punch bowl on the table and tips the box of
hard-boiled eggs into it.

                    SHARK
          Now Dorothy, I'm feeling generous.
          Here's your challenge.

Shark flexes a hundred dollar bill and places it on the
table next to the bowl of boiled eggs. The Children cheer.
Shark checks his watch.

                    SHARK
          Now you have 2 minutes to bob and
          spit. No swallowing now. Go!

Dorothy dunks efficiently, coming up with an egg in her
mouth and blows it out. She dunks, splashes and bobs again.

Screams of excitement from children.

                    SHARK
          Tick tick tick! You must all stay
          very quiet while mummy does her
          trick or you forfeit the cash ok.

The Children fall quiet.

Dorothy bobs. A look of excitement on her face. Water shoots
from her nose. A real dead man's eyeball looks out through
her teeth. The children SCREAM hysterically. Dorothy
SCREAMS; the retina hangs like a red tadpole.

INT.   SAN DIEGO COUNTY   OCEANSIDE SAFE HOUSE   NIGHT

Shark and Alex talk.

> SHARK
> Who wears the scariest mask? Every
> killer has an inner need to
> masquerade; even a super hero has
> an alter ego; another identity.

> ALEX
> The Hockey mask in 'Jason-X', Leather
> face in 'Texas Chainsaw massacre'?

> SHARK
> And the one used by Artist Edvard
> Munch?

> ALEX
> Pronounced 'monk'.  The one used in
> **'Scream'**?

> SHARK
> Yeah. It's not the mask that's
> scary it's the big fucking blade in
> his hand! Nothing to do with the
> mask. You'd shit it. Just like
> 'Psycho'. His mother's dry body in
> the chair. 'Hollow Man'. What's his
> name? The guy out of **'Footloose'**?

> ALEX
> Kevin Bacon.

> SHARK
> Yeah. Mr. Bacon. They pour pink goo
> all over his face which itself is
> suffocating. Ever had a mask made
> that way? You gotta experience it.

SOON LATER

Alex in a swivel chair, head back, bites down upon a
snorkel. Shark holds a jar of Vaseline, Alex hums in
disapproval.

                SHARK
Do I look like an ass bandit? It's
for your eyebrows. Stops the latex
sticking. I have morals.

Shark pours a bucket of pink creamy latex over Alex's face,
and with a spatula smears it just like one would ice a cake.

                SHARK
Hmmm. I was not exactly going for
the Darth Maul look.

Shark holds a chef's icing tube and reapplies the goo.

                SHARK
YES! Oh no, hold on, I'll try that
again. Practice makes perfect.

A motley set of ugly masks wrap around three mannequin
heads.

                SHARK
Try, try and try again. I didn't
say that I was an expert.

                ALEX
Looks like that splatter punk band.
'Slipnot'.

                SHARK
That's it! Who needs an alibi when
every 'Slipnot' freak out there can
be a suspect? Even some more
eligible than yourself.

Rubs chin with eureka expression on his face.

                ALEX
Genius, pure genius. Either that or
we're both mad.

                SHARK
'Slipnot' are geniuses. Or is that
geni-eye?

EXT.   FAIRGROUND   FERRIS WHEEL   NIGHT

Alex and Shark swing in a cradle atop the ride.

> SHARK
> Recklessly killing just makes a
> person another killer. A serial
> killer has the same modus operandi,
> kills the same way, like 'The Boston
> Strangler', strangling.

> ALEX
> Toni Curtis?

> SHARK
> I'm impressed.

> ALEX
> Was easy, they're doing a horror
> season on 'Channel 12'.


EXT.   FAIRGROUND   BUMPER CARS   NIGHT

Alex chauffeurs Shark around the circuit.

In a rival car, CO-ED#1 drives and CO-ED#2 in baseball cap,
the passenger.

Alex and Shark receive a sideswipe off the duo who holler to
their COLLEGE FRIENDS jeering from the ride's perimeter.

> SHARK
> That kid's notching up some bad
> Karma.

Alex sideswipes the Co-eds.

> CO-ED#1
> Bitch. That your Pops?

Shark grins.

EXT.    FAIRGROUND    GHOST TRAIN    NIGHT

CACKLES and SCREAMS from ride. In queue stand the Co-ed duo.

Shark bungs the RIDE OPERATOR a few bucks and with candy
floss in hand jumps into the next cart with Alex.

>                    CO-ED#1
>          Hey, that aint fair. Ever heard of
>          a queue?

>                    CO-ED#2
>          Candy floss?
>               (holding crotch)
>          Suck on this.

>                    SHARK
>               (to Alex)
>          Ready?

Both pull 3-D glasses out of their breast pocket and put
them on.

>                    ALEX
>          In 'Dolby 3-D Surround'.

Bright white teeth shine in the fluorescent light. Their car
crashes through the entrance door.

>                    SHARK
>          MUHAHAHAH! MUMMY!

MOMENTS LATER - EERIE CACKLES and SCREAMS.

Two CO-EDS sip milkshakes in the next cart; they pull faces
at COLLEGE FRIENDS who wait in the queue.

The RIDE OPERATOR checks their lap restraints.

>                    CO-ED#1
>          Yeah whatever.

                         CO-ED#2
              See you on the other side. Muhaha!
              I'm really scared.

Their bright white teeth shine in the fluorescent light.
Their car crashes through the entrance door.

Eerie noises from ride. O.S. Shark CACKLES, Alex SCREAMS.

An empty car crashes out through the exit and comes to a
halt. The restraint bar hangs in the air.

O.S. EERIE NOISES from Alex and Shark.

Co-eds SCREAM.

                         CO-ED#1 (O.S.)
              HELP US! Argh!

                         CO-ED#2 (O.S.)
              MUMMY!

                         SHARK
              Yeah-yeah, whatever.

A car crashes out through the exit and comes to rest.

Co-ed#1 wears 3-D glasses, an axe sticks out of his head.
Co-ed#2 shakes the restraint bar hysterically and SCREAMS.

LATER

Shark and Alex walk away from the rear of the 'Ghost Train'.
Two latex masks with snorkels poke out of a bin.

SCREAMS from the 'Ghost Train' in the distance.

                         SHARK
              Been a good night kid.

Alex bangs a newly acquired baseball cap against her thigh.

                         ALEX
              We'll have to do this again
              sometime. Partners?

                         SHARK
              That's my girl. Too many youngsters
              these days underestimate family
              values.

Both raise a milkshake and SLURP.


EXT.    CADILLAC (SUBURBS)    NIGHT

Shark in the driver's seat. Alex holds the door ajar. She
looks Tomboyish with hair all up inside her baseball cap.

                         SHARK
              Wanna go for a ride?

Shark plops the keys in Alex's lap.

LATER

Alex drives, Shark passenger.

                         ALEX
              Where we going?

Shark licks a finger and in the air, points ahead.

                         SHARK
              Off to test a theory of mine.
              Anywhere between Lake Eerie and the
              Gulf of Mexico.

                         ALEX
              Is this a learning curve?

                         SHARK
              A steep one.

EXT.　　INTERSECTION　　PATROL CAR　　NIGHT

Two OFFICERS sip coffee and scoff doughnuts in their
L.A.P.D. patrol car.

                    OFFICER#1
          Night shift. An easy road to cover
          on night shift. Every hot head
          around knows we'll have their ass
          if they come down this route.

                    OFFICER#2
          Hence the easy shift?

OFFICER#1 folds arms and closes eyes.

                    OFFICER#1
          That's right.

A car speeds past like lightning. Both exchange a look of
disbelief. The WOW-WOW siren comes on and lights spin
electric blue.

                    OFFICER#1
          In pursuit of speeding vehicle
          'Route 10' heading west out of Santa.

SCREECH of wheels gaining traction.

ONE MILE LATER

They speed past a parked-up Cadillac. SCREECH of brakes.
They reverse and shine a light at the car. Alex and Shark
wave from the rear seat.

                    OFFICER#1
          God I hate fags.

Alex removes her baseball cap letting her long hair flow.

Officer#1 takes notes. Officer#2 flicks his Nazi-like lamp
from Alex to Shark.

> OFFICER#1
> So let me get this straight. You
> weren't driving and you weren't
> driving either?

Shark and Alex remain still.

> OFFICER#1
> Let me guess. The driver ran away?

> SHARK
> That is a leading question, but
> yes, that's correct Officer.

> OFFICER#2
> (to Alex)
> So, you weren't driving?

Alex shakes head.

> OFFICER#2
> (to Shark)
> And you weren't driving?

> SHARK
> Well done Columbo. They should
> promote you.

Officer#2 leans back.

> OFFICER#2
> Lock 'em up!

INT.    POLICE STATION    NIGHT

Led by OFFICER#2 to a communal cell where every kind of 'Hobo'
and scummy low-life stay warm for the night.

> SHARK
> A warm towel and top bunk by the
> window please.

                    ALEX
          The facilities are criminal. What
          is this, the 'Bates Motel?'

Clocking the sink that someone has shit in.

                    SHARK
          On suite. Nice.
                    (to Officer#2)
          Breakfast seven-thirty? No sooner,
          I do not want you disturbing my
          letter to the 'Good Tour Guide'.


INT.    SAN DIEGO COUNTY    OCEANSIDE SAFE HOUSE    DAY

Shark eats toast. Alex places a few more slices onto the
plate.

                    SHARK
          My momma used to make the best
          marmalade. The strands, the little
          orange bits were a bit of a chew-on
          but beyond that, she was a great
          cook.

                    ALEX
          Is committing crime easy?

                    SHARK
          Crime, like marmalade, has a
          flavor. Getting away with it. Not
          having chewy bits, is the craft.

                    ALEX
          Nice metaphor.

                    SHARK
          Thanks, I'm working on them. I was
          the librarian in charge of book
          acquisitions at San Quentin prison.

INT.    SAN QUENTIN RIOT    CELL    DAY, MEMORY

THREE TATTOOED THUGS hold SHIVs to the GOVERNOR's throat.
Shark wheels in a trolley of books.

CLOSE ON BIBLE: Shark kisses it and takes a Derringer pistol
from within the hollow compartment.

           SHARK (V.O.)
     Let's just say the meek are blessed.
     God looks after them in mysterious
     ways.

BANG BANG BANG!


BACK TO SAFEHOUSE...


           SHARK
     Call me shallow but I still find
     that an attractive dust-cover makes
     or breaks a book.

Alex slaps a Monkey-Wrench in her palm.

           ALEX
     30's 'Silver Screen' gangsters always
     crack skulls with a 'Monkey-Wrench'.

           SHARK
     Try a vase, it's more you. No-one
     expects to be beaten to death by
     a pretty flower.


INT.    SAN DIEGO COUNTY    SAFE HOUSE    DAY, DAYDREAM

MUSIC: 'Adagio for strings' from PLATOON

Shark holds a vase above Alex's head and smashes it against her neck
causing her to fall unconscious.

INT.   SAN DIEGO COUNTY   OCEANSIDE SAFE HOUSE   DAY

Alex jumps to her feet.

Shark runs a finger around the plate, licks fingers and
brushes off breadcrumbs.

> SHARK
> Delicious. In this business, you
> have to be on top of all your
> faculties. Make real that dream.
> I'm setting up a deal up-north.
> Well, Canada. I want you to take
> care of this little city for me,
> call it a franchise. How's that
> sound?

> ALEX
> You're going where?

> SHARK
> Canada. Don't worry kid. I got
> dreams too. Don't let me cramp your
> style.

Pats Alex on the back. Reaches into coat. Tosses Alex some
keys that she catches.

CLOSE ON: Fob. 23A Hollow Point Drive, Santa Monica, C.A.

BACK TO SCENE

> SHARK
> Don't forget to clean the pool.

> ALEX
> Yeah, the filter.

> ALEX (V.O.)
> One second he was there, the next,
> he was gone.

> ALEX
> (juggles keys)
> To the bat cave.

INT.    SAN DIEGO COUNTY    OCEANSIDE SAFE HOUSE    NIGHT

Shark flicks the remote. FOOTBALL fills the TV screen.

> SHARK
> 'Channel 12' did you say?

STOCK SHOT:'The Body Snatchers', Donald Sutherland sleeps. A humanoid figure shakes as it grows from an organic pod.

> SHARK
> I'm a bit sleepy!

Alex comes into the living room. Shark mirrors what's on the screen by shaking in the chair.

Alex takes the remote and clicks it up a channel.

> ALEX
> That isn't twelve.

Shark ceases shaking and crosses his legs towards the TV.

> SHARK
> What a classic. Alien genocide
> that's what that is. Quite
> disturbing, but it is organic.

He shudders.

> ALEX
> Nothing a bit of pesticide couldn't
> solve.

> SHARK
> That's insects, you mean herbicide,
> weed killer. Herbicide is for
> plants.

> ALEX
> Yeah. You know what I mean.

EXT.    SUBURBAN HOUSE    DAY

Snow lay on the ground. SOUND: TRICKLE of pee. Alex behind a
weird elephant mask shuffles and slides skirt back down.

                         SHARK (V.O.)
                    Eventually everyone has to take a
                    leak. That piss-hole may be your
                    downfall.


INT.    POLICE STATION    LOST AND FOUND DEPT    DAY

Alex knocks. A SECRETARY opens a hatch beside the door.

                         SECRETARY
                    Yes? Can I help you?

                         ALEX
                    I seemed to have lost my pet and I
                    was wondering if he'd been handed in.

                         SECRETARY
                    Pet? In the lost and found?

                         ALEX
                    His name is "CUJO".

                         SECRETARY
                    Cujo? Ah!
                         (shouts behind)
                    Cujo's owner.
                         (back to Alex)
                    Bad news I'm afraid.

Blank look. Alex shows her photo I.D.

                         ALEX
                    Local Pool Attendant.

The main door opens and two burly OFFICERS appear. One holds
a plastic bag of yellowish fluid containing a dead Piranha.

                         OFFICER#1
                    Found at a crime scene.

He inspects the label, which reads "CUJO". A dead Piranha
floats on its side.

                    ALEX
          Cujo was found at a crime scene?
          Why would someone kill Cujo?

Officer#2 stifles a chuckle.

                    OFFICER#1
          We didn't find any prints on your
          bag, it's clean.

                    OFFICER#2
               (to Officer#1)
          I'll leave the paperwork to you.
          We shan't be needing Cujo's fin
          print.

                    ALEX
          I mean, if you need a statement
          I'll make one.

                    OFFICER#1
          I don't know much about tropical
          fish but I do know this breed is
          freshwater. Pond water can't have
          been any good for his gills.

Alex stares at the yellow liquid and nods.

                    ALEX
          Thank you officers.

INT.    POLICE STATION    LADIES BATHROOM    DAY

Alex pierces the bag, lets the fluid flow into the toilet.
Cujo plops into the bowl. Pulls chain and Cujo spirals away.

                    ALEX
          Bon voyage my piss-hole in the
          snow.

                    ALEX (V.O.)
          They didn't even arrest me for
          taking the piss. Antarctica
          tactics, that's what Shark calls
          them. Explorers visiting the colder
          extremities of our planet have to
          take their number two's home in a
          bag. That's why the countries so
          close to the 'pole are full of shit.


INT.    TELEVISION SHOP    DAY

Alex watches the 'Men's 100M **Freestyle**' on a super-sized TV.

Shark loiters between two buxom ASSISTANTS. A "SATISFACTION
GUARANTEED" banner hangs above his head.

                    ALEX
          Haha! Would you look at that.

Shark skips to her side.

CLOSE ON TV: **Swimmers bend; then launch into the pool.**

                    ALEX
          Olympic sized package?

                    SHARK
          Don't they know it. Go girl.
                    (beat)
          Oh. You mean the subscription?

Buxom ASSISTANT comes over. Shark bites his lip.

                         ASSISTANT#1
          The Olympic-ness of the screen
          kinda hits you in the face. Can
          almost smell the chlorine. Our
          deluxe model.


                         SHARK
          All the mod-cons in all the right
          places, aint she?


                         ASSISTANT#1
          Satisfaction guaranteed.


EXT.   ORANGE COUNTY   "WILD WILLIES" WATER PARK   DAY

Alex looks up to the top of the WATERSLIDE.

TOP OF RIDE

Shark sports a dorsal fin atop his swimming cap. Victoria in
lavender bikini waits behind him in the queue. She WINKS.

                         SHARK
            Please, before me. There's no rush.

She glances back at him, giggles flirtasciously and touches
her toes. Her bikini briefs nip between her butt cheeks.

                         SHARK
                    (hums the jaws tune)
            Dun-dun der-ra, dun-dun der-ra.

She pushes off and gravity takes her away.

Dons his 3-D glasses.

                         SHARK
            Classic.

**POOLSIDE** - Victoria massages a steroid BODYBUILDER.

BOTTOM OF RIDE - Alex watches a Shark's fin cruise the
shallows.

Shark rises from the water still wearing his 3-D's.

> SHARK
> I know her type, just playing the
> game, she knows 'Moby' here's a five
> course meal but she's holding out
> for a bit of 'Free Willy'.

Bodybuilder flexes, jogs up the steps that climb the ride.

> SHARK
> It moves.

> ALEX
> Meet you in the car park.

> SHARK
> Haha. A plan? Okey dokey. He's got
> a bit of a head start on you.

TOP OF RIDE

BODYBUILDER POV: launching himself down the tube.

> BODYBUILDER
> Weeeee!

CLOSE ON: Alex with axe pierces the underside of the tube.

IN TUBE: Water passes over it like a Shark's fin.

BACK TO SCENE

The Bodybuilder slides with legs wide open.

ALEX POV: A silhouette in the tube passes over the axe
blade.

> BODYBUILDER
> AAAAAAAARGHHH!

BOTTOM OF RIDE - A pair of torn trunks float amidst a bloody
pool. Victoria drops her beauty pageant persona and stares
coldly at the water.

Alex whistles calmly on her way to the car park.

                    ALEX
          Writers carry a notepad; I carry an
          axe, to capture those inspirational
          moments when you just need to let
          those creative juices flow.

EXT.    L.A.    PEACE AWARENESS LABYRINTH AND GARDENS    DAY

Alex attends the hedge with a pair of electric sheers.
PENSIONERS sip drinks at a table where Shark offers
refreshments.

                    SHARK
          Grand Prize fifty bucks. First to
          get out alive gets a T-shirt.

T-shirt logo: 'Anywhere but the face.'

                    SHARK
          Drink up, you'll need all your
          energy. Glucose enriched.

One WOMAN opens her purse.

                    SHARK
          On the house my lady.

Ushers them along.

                    SHARK
          Chop chop if you want to be in with
          a chance. Those cheats with maps
          will have to hand them in or they
          forfeit the T-shirt.

Takes maps off Pensioners who voluntarily hand them over.

                    SHARK
          Hey, what's that in your bag?

Snatches map from bag.

                    SHARK
          You're keen, you cheat. Now get in
          there with the rest of them.
                    (to Alex)
          Treat them mean keep them keen.

Alex uncovers a Chainsaw and hands it to Shark.

INT.    DOWNTOWN L.A.    THERAPIST OFFICE    DAY

Alex reclines. Therapist reads notes.

>               THERAPIST
> So, two men called. Looking like
> Mormons? He said,"we are here to
> spread the word of God." God's love
> as written in the book of Mormon?

>               ALEX
> Yeah that's right and I started to
> tell my story just the way it
> happened. (beat)"One night, this
> figure appeared in my room. Being
> quite spiritual, I waited, but it
> was a burglar! Luckily, I was in
> bed with my axe."

>               THERAPIST
> In bed with your axe?


INT.    HOUSE    DAY, MEMORY

MORMONS chat to Alex.

>               MORMON#1
> Your axe?

>               ALEX
> Ex! I was in bed with my ex.

>               MORMON#1
> I thought you said axe?

Alex laughs.

>               ALEX
> Freudian slip.
> I'll have to write that down. Axe?
> That's a good one. No. My ex! Not
> with him anymore, long story.

Mormon#1 looks at his watch.

                         MORMON#1
                    (nervously)
          We will have to be off. We have
          another appointment. We should be going.
          Can we dedicate a prayer to you?


                         ALEX
          Sure. You're not giving up on me
          are you? I recently felt an energy
          telling me I should have a
          boyfriend but now I'm doubling the
          energy up into a career move.
          Crossed fingers. Can we all pray
          that I can waltz into a real good
          job? Corporate? I'm just raking
          leaves off pools at the moment.

                         MORMON#1
          Sure.


The Mormons bow their heads.

Alex holds an axe behind the closing door.


INT.    SAN DIEGO COUNTY    OCEANSIDE SAFE HOUSE    DAY

Shark draws a cutthroat through the shaving foam covering
his neck.

                         SHARK
          Classic Sweeney Todd, real close
          shave. Now Sweeney Todd knew how to
          give a good clean cut. He was a
          Barber in London, the 'Demon
          Barber' you may have heard of him?

Looks to Alex who shakes head.

> SHARK
> Nice little swindle he had going
> on. Go in for "a short back and
> sides" and you come out next door in
> mince pies. A tasty little venture.

> ALEX
> What?

Shark draws blade further down his neck.

> SHARK
> Sat comfortably? Those were his
> words. He'd slit your throat and
> pull a lever that would deliver you
> to the cellar. If the cut didn't
> kill you, smashing your skull upon
> the basement floor would. Mrs. Todd
> next door sold the most delectable
> pies. Can you see where this is
> going?

> ALEX
> I'm no good with pastry.

Shark laughs.

> SHARK
> No you Dufus. We become partners.
> Keep it in the family, profit from
> it. Serial-killers and assassins
> never kill themselves. They all
> profit, be it for money or
> emotional kicks. Take your time,
> profit from crime, think about it.
> No 'nine to five', no contracts to
> sign no dotted line.


INT.    SAN DIEGO COUNTY    OCEANSIDE SAFE HOUSE    DAY, LATER

Semi-clad Shark shaves his armpits. Alex looks away.

> SHARK
> It's for hygiene. Plus hairs fall
> out all over the place. I don't mind
> my-place but when it's a murder
> scene that's 'D' 'N' all the w-'A'
> to prison. I'm no Chippendale.

Alex picks up a book from the occasional table. Flips it to
see the front and back cover.

> ALEX
> 'The Art of War?'

> SHARK
> Sun Tzu's 'The Art of War'. A
> classic! If a person writes a book
> called 'The Art of War' and you're
> into killing, death and murder
> that's a book for you. If you're a
> hired gun and you aint read it...
>         (taps head)
> ...you're short in the Mahogany
> department.
>         (points to Alex)
> Stealth, evasion, it's in there. A
> professional soldier's wet dream.
> Every MERC's bible.

Alex takes a seat, kicks off shoes and lifts feet onto the
table. Shark continues to shave, watches in the mirror.

> SHARK
> Most books are dog-eared about an
> inch in where the reader has
> stopped reading. Not that book. I
> must have read it at least twice
> this month.

> ALEX
> It's a library book!

> SHARK
> Yeah, true. But I know exactly
> where it is when I need it. I know
> exactly when the book was taken out
> and for how long and by whom.

                    ALEX
          You can deduce all that from this
          book?

                    SHARK
          No. Victoria deals with INTEL. Any
          record, data, that type o'shit
          know-it-all! Knowledgeable, keen,
          quick and dare I say, fit. She's a
          mean female data number crunching
          machine, with hips.

                    ALEX
          You're encourageable.

                    SHARK
          Work hard, play harder. She's
          dynamite. Did you say encourageable
          or incorrigible? 'Cause that means
          incapable of being corrected or
          reformed. One day the dictionary
          fell open on that one.

Eureka expression upon Alex's face.

                    ALEX
          Classic!

                    SHARK
          Alleged Contractors, the pea
          shooting boy scouts hanging from
          girders in Basra, 'Whitewater' MERC's
          in need of reading Sun Tzu's bible.
          (beat) "A sword makes a warrior as
          much--"

                    ALEX
          "--as a feather in your hair makes
          you an eagle?" Confucius.

                    SHARK
          Now that's one classic!

INT.   MEMORIAL PARK   ST.PETER'S EPISCOPAL CHURCH   DAY

WORSHIPERS kneel; each mouth opens to receive a circle of bread. VICAR places bread on their tongue and moves to the next…

> VICAR IS HENRY
> The body of Christ.

NEXT, Victoria, sporting a lavender blue hairnet.

> HENRY
> The body of Christ.

The bread touches her tongue. His index finger lingers, circles her lips. She looks up, smiles, the tip of her tongue dancing over the bread then the length of his finger.

> HENRY
> Oh my.
>      (coughs)
> Body of Christ!

NEXT PERSON

> HENRY
> The body of Christ.

Victoria gives a sideward glance. Henry by accident pokes the next person in the eye with a piece of bread.

LATER

Henry shakes the hand of Revelers who leave the Church. Victoria holds his hand and pouts.

> HENRY
> Confessions, six 'till late. For
> those feeling a little devilish.

INT.   HOTEL ANAHEIM   SWIMMING POOL   DAY, DAYDREAM

Alex sits on a highchair overlooking a private pool. FATHER
and SON approach her.

                    FATHER
          He likes it warm. He hates tepid it
          aint good for his skin. My boy's
          very particular.

                    ALEX
          I'll turn the heat up. Just one
          rule, no running beside the pool.

Father and son descend into pool.

Alex raises her 3D glasses and smiles. Alex's hand hovers
over a remote with a bright red button.

                    ALEX
          May get a bit 'nippy.'

She presses the button.

STOCK FOOTAGE: School of Piranha frenzying around a carcass,
they pick it clean to the bone.

BACK TO SCENE


INT.   ST.PETER'S EPISCOPAL CHURCH   CONFESSION BOX   DAY

An ornate grill separates Victoria from Henry.

                    HENRY (O.S.)
          I think she's as ready as she'll
          ever be.

                    VICTORIA
          We'll soon see.

LATER

Alex peers through the grill; she can see the whiteness of
Henry's dog collar. Alex reclines, lounges with her feet up
the wall.

> HENRY (O.S.)
> Leaders with long careers lead from
> the back. Only fools rush in; for
> instance, the Alamo, Omaha,
> warriors to the front, leaders to
> the rear. If any survive, then they
> too become heroes. Yeah, one in a
> million. For now, I'm satisfied
> with just small jobs, later, maybe
> a long successful corporate career
> lay ahead. There's a lot of leeway
> for lateral movement at the back.
> Left, right, dig in, crawl under if
> need be. Think about it. Who did
> you last hide behind?

> ALEX
> Is this in Sun Tzu's 'Art of Hiding?'

> HENRY (O.S.)
> Kinda, it's called 'stealth.' You can
> still be at the front and live if
> you use stealth. If someone's been
> there, and they're giving you
> advice in how not to get your ass
> blown off, listen to them, for
> those who've been clearly within an
> inch of heaven and got the fuck
> outta there share wise words.

BOTH EXIT CONFESSION BOX

Both Henry and Alex wear 3-D glasses. They point at each
other in recognition of like-minds.

> ALEX
> Smelt a little of lavender in
> there.

INT.   MALIBU COLONY   CONDO (OVERLOOKING SAFEHOUSE)   DAY

All-black MOBSTER pokes his binoculars through a kink in the
blinds. FATSO points a state-of-the-art pistol at a TV set

                    MOBSTER
          Just some kid in a baseball cap
          cleaning the pool.

CLOSE ON: TV set. Contestant presses BUZZER.

                    TV HOST
          The first man in space.

BACK TO SCENE

                    MOBSTER
          Who is Neil Armstrong?

                    TV HOST (O.S.)
          The first man in space?

                    CONTESTANT (O.S.)
          Who is Uri Gagarin, Major.

                    FATSO
          Unlucky.

                    MOBSTER
          So it wasn't... Who is Armstrong,
          Neil, Commander?

                    FATSO
          Next you'll be saying it's Colonel
          Steve Austin. You'll be saying he
          went to the moon too.

                    MOBSTER
          The Six Million Dollar Man? Come in
          FABER THREE and all that. At his
          best, like you, runs in slow
          motion.

A red dot from Fatso's pistol shines upon the back of
Mobster's head.

EXT.    OCEANSIDE SAFE HOUSE    DAY

Fatso and Mobster ring the front door bell, Bibles in hand.

> MOBSTER
> I still don't think this'll work.

Alex opens the door.

> FATSO "JOHNSON"
> Morning sir. My name is Elder
> Johnson and this is Elder
> Armstrong. Messengers spreading the
> loving word of god.

> ALEX
> Come in. Forgive me for not shaking
> your hands I'm just cleaning the
> pool. Tea? Coffee?

> MOBSTER "ARMSTRONG"
> Two sugars, please.

Alex raises a brow.

> FATSO "JOHNSON"
> Milk, one sugar.

> ALEX
> Please take a seat.

INT.    OCEANSIDE SAFE HOUSE    DAY

A tea service sits on a tray on the table. Fatso and Mobster
lay comatose, both foam at the mouth.

> ALEX (V.O.)
> Only Mormons use the name Elder,
> and they don't drink tea or coffee.
> Whereas' the morons,'pool cleaner'
> washed their dirty mouths out.
> Keeping L.A. clean can be MURDER.

EXT.    OCEANSIDE SAFE HOUSE    POOL    DAY

A rope binds Alex's hands to an anchor behind her back. BOSS
motions the diving board at the deep end.

                    BOSS
          Get walking. It's the plank for you
          girl.

Alex plummets off the board to the bottom of the pool.

                    BOSS
          Girl overboard. S.O.S. Someone call
          the 'Pool Attendant'.

A life ring lands in the pool.

                    BOSS
          What a pity.


INT.    OCEANSIDE SAFE HOUSE    POOL    DAY

Alex POV looking up at the floating ring.


INT.    DOWNTOWN L.A.    THERAPIST OFFICE    DAY, MEMORY

Alex stares at the textured PLASTER on the ceiling that
reminds her of the Moon's *Sea of Tranquility*.


EXT.    OCEANSIDE SAFE HOUSE    POOL    DAY

Enter Henry behind Boss.

                    HENRY
          Even in the shallows you're 'way
          out of your depth' when there's
          a Shark around.

Henry holds a dog catching device, a pole with a lasso at
one end. The loop hooks over the Boss's head and tightens
into a strangle hold. Using leverage the Boss falls into the
pool.


INT.   DOWNTOWN L.A.    THERAPIST OFFICE    DAY, ALEX'S MEMORY
                                 ...AND PART HALLUCINATION


SECONDS EXPAND...

On the floor the choking Boss points his pistol towards
ceiling. Firing, the bullets appear as tiny comets rising to
the moon-like ceiling and parts of it chip away.


INT.   OCEANSIDE SAFE HOUSE    POOL    DAY

Alex's POV: Boss swallows water. He kicks out with his legs;
pinned by the pole held from above. He fires bullets from
the bottom of the pool. Each bullet creates a trail up to
the water's surface.


EXT.   OCEANSIDE SAFE HOUSE    POOL    DAY

Henry pulls Alex's limp body from the pool.

                    HENRY
          Alex! Alex!


                    HENRY (V.O.)
          Sometimes the end just doesn't feel
          like it should.


                    ALEX (V.O.)
          Those men who went to the moon had
          faith in something. Faith in
          humankind. God.

Alex's eyes open. She takes a calm breath of air.

                    ALEX
          I had faith in you.

Henry's lip curls.

                    ALEX
          You know you're quite something. My
          hero, a regular Johnny Weissmuller.

                    HENRY
          A classic.

                    ALEX
          Escaping the 'jaws of death.'

                    HENRY
          Let's not make it a regular thing eh?


INT.   SAN CLEMENTE   HOME   DAY, 20 YEARS EARLIER

Young Alex sits on the floor. A Mermaid adorns the cover of
a dot-to-dot coloring book in her Mother's hand.

                    ALEX (V.O.)
          Memories can be so colorful.

CLOSE ON: Mother's finger peels the paper from a purple
crayon.

                    ALEX (V.O.)
          The scent of a waxy blue crayon
          mixes with the memory of Mother's
          nail varnish.

                    MOTHER
          I will start you off.

She wiggles the crayon upon the page.

CLOSE ON: The crayon creates a blue ocean around a dot-to-
dot Shark.

>                    MOTHER (O.S.)
>          Blue for the ocean. Which color
>          shall we make the shark?
>
>                    YOUNG ALEX
>          They eat people. Red!
>
>                    ALEX (V.O.)
>          That was the beginning.
>          Something about stress and the
>          danger of the pool. We were too
>          young to understand. And with
>          little support, we were told we
>          were to go on a long journey.

EXT.   L.A.   SAN CLEMENTE   SUBURBAN GARDEN   DAY, MEMORY

Young Alex holds Mother's hand. Young Henry waves goodbye
from the rear window of a car that pulls away.

>                    ALEX (V.O.)
>          We didn't know what it meant. Our
>          descent into the pool. We didn't
>          know where we were going. Or when
>          we would be launched into the lives
>          we now lead. Our naivety and
>          feverish anticipation for adventure
>          catapulted us headlong towards the
>          dark side of the moon.

Young Alex stares.

INT.   SAN DIEGO COUNTY   OCEANSIDE SAFE HOUSE   DAY

Shark removes Alex's earphones.

>                    SHARK
>               (serious voice)
>          Alex. I have something to tell you.
>
>                    ALEX
>          Uh?

Shark crouches.

                    SHARK
          I tracked down your older brother.

                    ALEX
          Yeah?

                    SHARK
          I'm your brother, Alex. My little
          Pool Attendant.

Alex exhales through her nose, her chest cramps; she tries
best she can to stifle her tears.

                    ALEX (V.O.)
          It was as if the skies were
          clearing. The Sun had hidden behind
          the Moon for too long.

STOCK: The end of an eclipse, when the sun reappears.

                    SHARK IS HENRY
          Come on. The news aint all that
          bad.

Through tears and giggles.

                    ALEX
          You daft arse.

                    HENRY
          I think a celebration's in order!

Counts on his fingers.

                    HENRY
          Water world. Fairground. What's
          next?

                    ALEX
          Vegas?

In walks Victoria who deftly sets up her laptop.

                    VICTORIA
          Hi Alex, we have much to discuss.
          And a whole pool of dirty problems
          to filter. But first--


INT.   DOWNTOWN L.A.   THERAPIST OFFICE   DAY

Alex and Therapist.

                    ALEX
          I'm afraid this is my last session.
          I've come to say goodbye.

                    THERAPIST
          The door is always open Alex.

Shuffles patient's index cards.

                    THERAPIST
          And before you go.

                    ALEX
          Huh?

                    THERAPIST
          Your birthday Alex is the twentieth
          of November? Scorpio's element is
          water? Do you know your horoscope
          for tomorrow?

Look of enlightenment on Alex's face.

Therapist places a poster tube in her hand.

                    THERAPIST
          Go catch a wave.

Alex smiles.

                    ALEX
          Thank you, I will.

EXT.   LA   METROLINK (MOVING)   DAY

Henry and Victoria face Alex who opens a POSTER tube
revealing a poster of the 'CRATERS OF THE MOON'.

> HENRY
> Victoria our Mission Director.
> I know you've met.

> VICTORIA
> You've great ideas Alex. Contracts
> with no dotted-line and nowhere to
> sign. Call it an exclusive family
> venture.

EXT.   L.A.   SOMEWHERE IN THE MALIBU COLONY   DAY

Alex drags a net across the surface of a swimming pool.
A single leaf floats out of reach.

> VICTORIA (V.O.)
> Brother and sister; formidable,
> unorthodox; their strengths
> complementing their weaknesses.

Henry with harpoon at the hip takes aim and blasts the leaf
from the water.

> ALEX (V.O.)
> Got a problem?

> HENRY (V.O.)
> Got a dirty job?

> VICTORIA (V.O.)
> Call the Pool attendant.

> VICTORIA
> Guys.

Henry looks over his shoulder. Victoria holds a 'Polaroid
instamatic camera'.

(OVER) *WE DONT NEED ANOTHER HERO* - TINA TURNER

*Footnote: p.81/82 "With music the final pages still make me cry. " - Karl, the author.*

                        VICTORIA
            Say cheese.

              ALEX                    HENRY
         Cheese!                 Cheese!

CLICK-CLICK - CLOSE ON: Old Polaroid of Young Henry in a
N.A.S.A. spacesuit with Young Alex beside.

EVEN CLOSER: Young Alex's GREEN EYES

                        MATCH CUT to ALEX (Alexandra Vino):

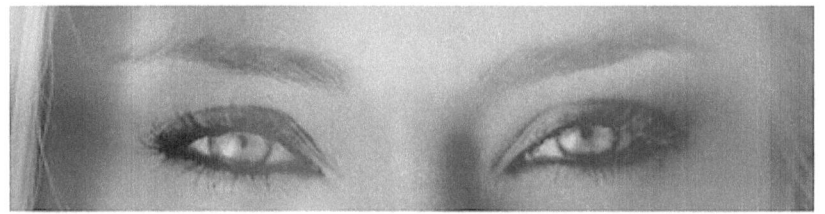

**FLASHBACK:**    EXT.    NEW YORK CITY    GROUND ZERO    DAY, 9/11

Reveal Alex, a talc-like figure in the fog. The YELLOW
PIPING on her uniform shows her to be an FDNY fire fighter.

Lattice-like remains of the World Trade Centre jut to the
heavens behind her.

Masses of dust obscure the SUN.

Morph SUN into a NEGATIVE MOON with a rippling pool beneath.

                    ALEX (V.O.)
            If life tries to break you; don't
            shoot for anything other than the
            Moon. This is just the beginning.

                    THE END

                                        FADE OUT:

            TEASER FOLLOWS...

"L.A. SERIAL POOL" TV SERIES

<u>TEASER</u>

FADE IN:

EXT.   COORS FIELD   DENVER   NIGHT, WORLD SERIES

Whip around roaring crowd, heady mixture of colors. STADIUM
JINGLE builds to a crescendo.

Batter "GARRETT ATKINS" taps the mound.

Pitcher "HIDEKI OKAJIMA" winds up, behind him a Tomboyish
umpire, ALEX in baseball cap draws a pistol from the hip.

BALL POV from PITCHER'S HAND to SWINGING BATTER.

SNAP to POV of WHIZZING BULLET overtaking BALL.

BANG-BANG-BANG

                                                    FADE TO BLACK:

                        SHARK (V.O.)
                Three strikes and you're out.

FADE IN 'SERIAL POOL' LOGO a NEGATIVE MOON with a rippling
pool beneath.

                        ALEX (V.O.)
                Killing people is easy. Getting
                away with it can be just murder.

                        THE END

                                                    FADE OUT:

                <u>END OF TEASER</u>

"L.A. SERIAL POOL"

EPISODIC BIBLE

Created by

Karl Smith

Early draft...

Alex was originally Henry's younger brother.

The decision to make Alex female was easily made when actress Alexandra Vino became interested.

"I love this project... the actions of the Principals goes from crazy to crazier.
Empathizing, wanting to give them a hug is the craziest thing."
- Karl Smith

# L.A. SERIAL POOL

## *"Murder in the fourth"*

'Getting the story straight'

### CONTENTS

# L.A. SERIAL POOL

## *"Murder in the fourth"*

Introduction:

Continually seeking escapism by pressing the TV remote?
*Serial Pool* <u>is</u> 'the attractive fantasy' you seek.

Share laughter and tears in this ultra adventure where
principals survive by the skin of their teeth. Buckle-up
for non-stop nail biting action.

Are you a Producer? Director? Network? Print me out. Take
me home. Give me some loving.

To the prosperous future of *Serial Pool*.

                                              - Karl Smith


OVERVIEW:

Feature: Serial Pool Attendant written by Karl Smith.

Series title: L.A. Serial Pool
Pilot episode: Murder in the fourth

<u>Type of Material: Television one-hour</u>

| | |
|---|---|
| Title: | L.A. Serial Pool |
| Number of Pages: | 42+ per episode |
| Author: | Karl Smith |
| Publisher/Date: | |
| Submitted to: | Library Of Congress Aug 2008 |
| Circa: | Present |
| Location: | LA + one SHOWCASE location/episode |
| Analyst: | |
| Category: | Crime |
| Date: | |
| Elements: | Horror/Crime/Drama |

SHOWCASE THE BEST OF THE USA via LOCATION
eg: The Hoover Dam.

## L.A. SERIAL POOL

### *"Murder in the fourth"*

**Genre:**
Crime Detective Horror

# SERIAL POOL ATTENDANT

Synopsis:
On an L.A. beach Alex (pool attendant) meets her idol, the notorious Shark (real name Henry, a high profile killer on parole).  Shark mentors Alex in the art of 'murder' and in 'not getting caught'. Cultural references lead to his catchphrase . . .

## "A CLASSIC!"

The big reveal: Shark is not just a serial killer but a puppet taking orders from Victoria (once screenplay tutor to Alex) and mission director of an assassin-like organisation known as the  . . .

### 'SERIAL POOL'

It is not mere chance that brings Alex and Henry together.

Siblings with a flair for death. Shark takes his sister under his wing.

Hitmen liaising as *real CLEANERS.*

### *"IF YOUR PROBLEM IS TOO BIG TO FILTER* ### *. . .YOU CALL THE POOL ATTENDANT"*

Concept:
Two loyal Psycho's team up to create the L.A. version of "Miami Vice".
Add a sexy mission director... Victoria... a prinkling of "Mission Impossible" and that's ENTERTAINMENT!

### *"YOU'LL DIE LAUGHING"*
*"...lunatic brother-sister psychology at its finest."*

...it's a killer Script!

**Premise:**
*'Miami Vice'* meets *'American Psycho'.*
Episode pilot is in four-act ONE-HOUR TV format aimed at:
Broadcast television networks (ABC, CBS, NBC; FOX) where Act breaks match the commercial breaks.

# L.A. SERIAL POOL

### *"Murder in the fourth"*

The Heroes Journey:

**Myths:**

- Myths give us our sense of personal identity, answering the question, "Who am I?"
- Myths make possible our sense of community. We are thinking mythically when we show loyalty to our town our nation or our team. Loyalties to our friends or community are the result of strong myths that reinforce social bonding.
- Myths are what lie underneath our moral values.
- Mythology is our way of dealing with the inscrutable mystery of creation and death.

**Elements that have to be there:**

- Establishing the hero's world
- The call to adventure
- Entering the mythological woods
- Trail of trials
- Encountering the evil one
- Gaining the hero's prize
- Returning that prize to the community

Example:

**Deconstruction of Million Dollar Baby** (Academy Award Winner Best Film, 2005):

- Call to Adventure:
- Refusal of the Call:
- First Threshold:
- Physical Separation (Belly of the Whale):
- Transformation (Road of Trials) x3:
- Seizing the Sword:
- Rebirth Through Death:
- Atonement
- Apotheosis: Maggie
- Ultimate Boon:
- Refusal of the Return:
- Magic Flight:
- Rescue from Without:
- Crossing the Return Threshold:
- Master of the Two Worlds:
- Freedom to Live:

# L.A. SERIAL POOL

### *"Murder in the fourth"*

Characters:

### Core 'Principals'

| | |
|---|---|
| ALEX (late 20's) | Lead actress.<br>Arc: Vulnerable, becoming audacious in her actions.<br>Easily led by stronger figures. |
| HENRY (30's)<br>AKA 'SHARK' | Older brother and wise-ass sidekick.<br>Arc: Confident, life-of-the-party, attention seeker.<br>Enjoys getting out of trouble as much as he likes getting into it. |
| VICTORIA (30's)<br>also BAG LADY | Sexy face of the 'Serial Pool' organization.<br>Arc: Spinsterish with integrity, retentively dotting the I's and crossing the T's. Always having done her homework she is always a step ahead of everyone. |

YOUNG HENRY (child)
YOUNG ALEX (few years younger)

### Recurring 'bit parts'

| | |
|---|---|
| FEATURE/SERIES BIG BOSS | Named Actor |

### Episode specific 'bit parts'

| | |
|---|---|
| EPISODIC CONTRACTOR | Working for BIG BOSS or VICTORIA |
| EPISODIC TARGET | Dies during Teaser |
| SOFT SUPPORT | ie Relative of TARGET/VICTIM |
| UNUSUAL KILLER | Dies during Episode |

### Location specific parts - Episode: Murder in the Fourth

RED SOX – PITCHER
BACKSTOP
ROOKIES – BATTER
SECOND
THIRD
CNN SPORTS CORRESPONDENT
CNN ANCHOR

# L.A. SERIAL POOL

## *"Murder in the fourth"*

Cast

Alex.................................ALEXANDRA VINO
Henry............................. BRIAN SPANGLER
Victoria..................................................

Big Boss..................................................

Writer/ Show Creator  .................. KARL PETER SMITH
Director..................................................
Producer..................................................
Executive Producer........................................
Music....................................................
Production Manager........................................
Script Editor............................................

Interested parties:
- ACTORS
  - L.A. based
- FUNDING
  - NZTE
- PRODUCTION COMPANY
  - 
- DIRECTOR(S)
  - RONALD JUDKINS (THE ATWATER COMPANY)

Artistic contributions:
Please contact - Karl Smith
orphichouse@yahoo.co.uk

If you would like to contribute in any way shape or form
then please feel free to drop me a line. Suggestions for
this project are more than welcome.

                                        - Karl Peter Smith

          Credit where credit is due.

# L.A. SERIAL POOL

### *"Murder in the fourth"*

Hero's journey formula

KEY
Page/minute - LOCATION
Essential element of HERO'S JOURNEY


p.2 EXT. STAKEOUT LOCATION #1 - DAY
(1) Establishing Heroes World eg: BASEMENT

p.7 INT. SAFE HOUSE - DAY
(2) Call to Adventure

p.9 EXT. MEETING PLACE - DAY
(3) Entering the Mythological Woods eg: Parent's Home

p.17 INT. STAKEOUT LOCATION #2 - DAY
(4) Trail of trials eg: MORGUE

p.18 INT. VICTORIA'S HOME - DAY
(4) Trail of trials

p.19 INT. ACTION LOCATION - NIGHT
(4) Trial (Obstacle resulting in Death) eg: Nightclub

p.24 INT. POLICE STATION - DAY
(4) Trail of trials (Obstruction)

p.25 EXT. STAKEOUT LOCATION #3 - DAY
(4) Trail of trials eg: ARCADE

p.35 INT. CONTRACTORS'S HOME - DAY
(4) Trail of trials (Stealthy/unseen) eg: APARTMENT

p.41 INT. PLACE OF PERIL - NIGHT
(4) Trial (Sense of foreboding) eg: Deserted building

p.43 INT. TARGET'S HOME - DAY
(5) Encounter the evil one.

p.54 INT. CONTRACTOR'S HOME (DESCENT) - DAY
(6) Gaining the Hero's prize Eg: LIFT, FIRE ESCAPE

(7) Returning that prize to the community

# L.A. serial pool

## L.A. SERIAL POOL

### *"Murder in the fourth"*

Occurrences:

KEY:
(*) LOGO & 5 MINUTE ACT BREAK
(-) TRANSITION SPIN CAMERA OVER L.A.

Page/minute

```
0-1 Previously on Serial Pool
1-4 24 HOURS EARLIER - EXT. STAKEOUT LOCATION #1 - DAY
        EXT. COORS FIELD
4-6 (-) INT. SAFE HOUSE - DAY
        INT. OCEANSIDE SAFEHOUSE (SAN DIEGO COUNTY)
6-9 (-) EXT. MEETING PLACE - DAY
        INT. RECORD STORE

9-14 *
14-15 INT. TECH DEPT (VICTORIA'S OFFICE) - DAY
        INT. TECH DEPT, MALIBU COLONY


15-16 CHILDHOOD FLASHBACK
        INT. THERAPIST'S OFFICE
16-18 EXT. STAKEOUT LOCATION #2 - DAY
18-20 POV SPIN OVER L.A. - INT. SAFE HOUSE - DAY
        INT. OCEANSIDE SAFEHOUSE (SAN DIEGO COUNTY)
20-22 INT. TARGET'S HOME - DAY
        INT. LOVELL BEACH HOUSE (NEWPORT BEACH)
22-23 INT. TARGET'S HOME (DESCENT) - DAY
        EXT. LOVELL BEACH HOUSE (NEWPORT BEACH)
23-25 INT. POLICE STATION - DAY
25-26 (-) INT. STAKEOUT LOCATION #3 - DAY
26-27 INT. VICTORIA'S HOUSE - DAY
27-28 INT. STAKEOUT LOCATION #3 - DAY
28-32 *
32-35 (-) INT. TECH DEPT (VICTORIA'S OFFICE) - DAY
35-36 INT. CONTRACTOR'S HOME - DAY
36-37 INT. VICTORIA'S OFFICE - DAY
37-37 EXT. MEETING PLACE - DAY
37-37 INT. SAFE HOUSE - DAY
        INT. OCEANSIDE SAFEHOUSE (SAN DIEGO COUNTY)
37-38 INT. TECH DEPT (VICTORIA'S OFFICE) - DAY
38-39 INT. VICTORIA'S OFFICE - DAY
39-39 CHILDHOOD FLASHBACK
40-42 INT. VICTORIA'S OFFICE - DAY
42-42 EXT. PLACE OF PERIL - NIGHT
42-42 EXT/INT. CONTRACTOR'S HOME - DAY
42-42 INT. TECH DEPT (VICTORIA'S OFFICE) - DAY
43-43 EXT/INT. TARGET'S HOME - DAY
```

# L.A. SERIAL POOL

### *"Murder in the fourth"*

```
43-48 *
48-50 (-)EXT. TARGET'S GARDEN - DAY
50-51 INT. PLACE OF PERIL - NIGHT
        MULTIPLE CHILDHOOD FLASHBACKS
51-52 INT. CONTRACTOR'S HOME - NIGHT
52-52 INT. CONTRACTOR'S (DESCENT) - NIGHT
52-54 EXT. TARGET'S HOME - NIGHT
54-57 INT. SAFE HOUSE - DAY
           INT. OCEANSIDE SAFEHOUSE (SAN DIEGO COUNTY)
```

58-58 2 weeks later HENRY (V.O) philosophical

# L.A. SERIAL POOL

## *"Murder in the fourth"*

<u>Budget considerations</u>:

<u>LOCATIONS</u>:
The STRUCTURE of the script allows for the opening
LOCATION to be the most exotic. There will be only <u>one</u>
per script and this location draws the audience in with
an episodic HOOK.

Referred to in the script as STAKEOUT LOCATION #1

The exotic location will be the cliff hanger location
taking the audience to the first ACT BREAK. A CLIP of the
location will be used to recap the location upon the
return to ACT TWO.

<u>NIGHT SCENES</u>:
To be shot INT. ON SET using controlled lighting to make
full use of the crew's normal working hours.

# L.A. SERIAL POOL

## *"Murder in the fourth"*

ONE-HOUR format.

The time breakdown with three six-minute breaks works like this:

| | |
|---:|:---|
| Teaser: | 1 page |
| Act One: | 8 pages |
| Act Two: | 13 pages |
| Act Three: | 13 pages |
| Act Four: | 8 pages |
| Tag: | 1 Page |
| Total: | 42 pages |

Teaser-Act One (6) Act Two (6) Act Three (6) Act Four-Tag = 60 mins total.

- EXAMPLE -

PREVIOUSLY:

- <u>Pilot Clips (Feature Format):</u> SERIAL POOL ATTENDANT

PILOT EPISODE:
- <u>(One-hour Format):</u> MURDER IN THE FOURTH

ACT I
o  Pre-emptive strike

ACT II
o  Bench the plan.

ACT III
o  Home Run

ACT IV
o  Queer eye for a bad guy

Three storylines run concurrently. The A story is the main plot, while the B story is the major subplot. The C story is called a runner or minor subplot, usually character developing. It usually occurs three/four times within the hour.

| STORY | BEATS |
|:---:|:---:|
| A | 12 |
| B | 8 |
| C | 4 |

# L.A. SERIAL POOL

### *"Murder in the fourth"*

Recurring ELEMENTS

TEASER:
SLOW MOTION SEQUENCE: ALEX delivers a killing blow.

CAMERA TAKES POV. The audience participate as a character
from the start.

HENRY CLEANS HANDS: A compulsive cleaning disorder is the
reason why Henry has avoided detection by the CSI crews
for so long.

DIALOGUE: Henry says "classic" once per episode.

SURREAL TEASER: A character animates out of character...
ie: BURLESQUE FANTASY: Victoria acts out in Alex's mind.

GUEST VIDEO: Guest Director. No dialogue. Featured track.
In a similar fashion to "Baywatch's" slow-motion except
this can be an up-tempo killer video sequence.

SHOWCASE THE BEST OF THE USA: via LOCATION
Inspiration from MEGA STRUCTURES ie: The Hoover Dam.

VICTORIA checks out the POOL of KILLERS cropping up on
her radar.

ALEX needs to pass her UCLA screenwriting course.
ALEX uses the lessons learnt in the episode to complete a
KILLER SCRIPT for her screenwriting course. Her TUTOR is
of course VICTORIA, the HEAD of the SERIAL POOL.

TAG:
MATCH CUT the final FADE OUT to the SERIAL POOL LOGO; the
negative moon above rippling water.
Psychologically internalizing the previously shown
external events played out upon the screen.

# L.A. SERIAL POOL

## *"Murder in the fourth"*

Script Analysis:

PLOT: Brother & sister work for a black ops organization. They have an unusual talent of killing and getting away with it. Their cover story...mere Pool Attendants.

THEME: As cold blooded killers, they sometimes warm to an enemy and make the moral decision of whether it is better to kill or recruit the enemy.

LOGIC: After finding his adopted sister Henry has to tackle the idea of having to kill someone else's.

EXPOSITION: Glimpses of a lost childhood filter through Alex's stories told from her shrink's settee.

COMPLICATION: Victoria feeds upon their search for acceptance, achieving the goal...be it a 'mere smile' from Victoria becomes more important than their own mortality.

TENSION: Putting the audience in the driving seat so that they themselves think "Could I escape this?"

MAIN QUESTION: Shall we kill MR. BIG? Or if he's like us, do we recruit him?

MAIN ACTION? Alex is an ex fire fighter, a survivor of 9/11. Her world is the real world in which we all live. Each episode I will teasingly draw the audience into a world where through insane situations all are teased into thinking for an hour at least that Alex is immortal.

CAUSE OF THE ACTION?: Victoria, a black ops operative gives the duo impossible missions.

RESULTING ACTION? The impossible hunt becomes a reality.

CONCLUSION? The impossible is achieved. Characters return to a lawful environment and the heroes will rest... ...until Victoria throws down the gauntlet once again.

PROTAGONIST? ALEX and HENRY

ANTAGONIST? Pick a face at home with the MOST WANTED.

MOST INTERESTING CHARACTER? Alex, Henry or Victoria.

# L.A. SERIAL POOL

Scene Analysis:      *"Murder in the fourth"*

**Previously:** (0-1) Tension "Previously"

**Teaser:** (1-2) Start with a teaser that illustrates the premise of the episode. It needs to show us this week's central problem and get the viewer to want to keep watching. Make sure it really does tease us by ending on a note of tension.

## ACT I
### Pre-emptive strike

**Act One:** Open Act One with a response to the teaser. It also works best if it too ends with tension. Depending on the kind of series this is, the tension can be personal and involve a series regular, or it can be something that is happening to a guest star. Main character statement (V.O.) Set up the goal for the character. Then your character runs into an obstacle. By the end of the act he should reach or fail to reach that immediate goal.

+2 Stakeout Location #1 ALEX, set scene, unusual perspective
+3 show Alex + Henry's face. The chase. Face of UNUSUAL KILLER
+4 Axe fight Alex vs. UNUSUAL KILLER. Henry Witty dialogue.
+5 Opening credits
+6 "Los Angeles" Street L.A Verbally set scene.
+7 Car Alex = Henry Highway Brief description of Suspect
+7 HENRY (Safe house)
+ 8 Highway BROTHER back-story blind folded, unaware of trouble.
+9 Struggle BIG BOSS kidnaps BROTHER...lead
BREAK (+10 +15)

## ACT II
### Bench the plan.

Act Two: complicate the character's mission, and then raise the stakes. Be sure to move your subplots forward as well and raise the stakes again. By this point, your character is at his lowest point. Begin Act Two with the aftermath or resolution of the previous tension and conclude with big trouble for the main hero or a regular. This keeps the reader turning pages.

+15 SUBURB SISTER (Meeting Place) FATHER "Words of affection"
+16 MOTHER cares. She defends Brother verbally TENSION back story
+17 COPS visit (Meeting Place) > (Stakeout Location #2) Brother Dead. Tattoo clue. Sister sobs in car. Persona; chat heart strings.
+18 Time lapse to nightfall. (Safe house) Tech report on TV about Brother
+19 Freeway INTRUDERS, (Action location) Use Technical Detection Device clue
+20 Weird scary location UFC JUMP+MELEE – TATTOOIST vs. A Witty Quip
+21 Brother's (Grave) Sister. Intimate voicemail memory, brother being further away
+22 (Target's Home) Quiet/personal affects - deduction
+23 A the intruder, Sister pursues (Target's Home descent), Alex shows weakness
+24 (Police Station) Sister COP File-brother is a suspect.
+25 Sister diversion
+26 Sister steals file
+27 Victoria techno talk explaining Serial Pool.

# L.A. SERIAL POOL

## *"Murder in the fourth"*

+28 Victoria + A leads on Brother? Magazine showing Brother's prowess.
+29 (Stakeout Location #3) Sister HOODY old bad friend of Brother – same tattoo
+30 Hoody escape Double cross
BREAK (+30 +35)

### ACT III
### Home run

**Act Three:** your character, hopefully, will have reached a new level of determination. You will have made things even tougher for him, so he'll have to dig inside himself for more strength. Be sure to deal with your subplots and tie up loose ends. Finally, is the resolution or pay-off. Resolve the previous problem in Act 3 and save the hero, and then end with the hero and his allies putting together all the pieces of whatever puzzle they've been trying to solve. Finish Act Three with a major crisis that leads to the climax of this episode.

+35 (Contractor's Home) Techno – Google – origins of Tattoo pic of Victoria.
+36 (Victoria's Office) Sister + Defensive VICTORIA 'hello'
+37 Victoria tells story of <u>new drug</u> to **Alex** expert on the unusual.
+38 ID's Tattoo and knows location of Big Boss's House.
+39 Night transition. Sister is car jacked.
+40 Whispering voice/phone call (O.S.) "Your brother" Sister led into (Place of Peril)
+41 Heartbeat inside (Place of Peril) UNUSUAL KILLER #2 Sister shoots it.
+42 H come to Sister's rescue. Witty line.
+43 Sister's impossible realization.
BREAK (+43 +48)

### ACT IV
### Queer eye for a bad guy

**Act Four:** The heroes come through in the nick of time.

+48 Alley Truck (Place of Peril) Mystery man…BIG BOSS
+49 (Professor's House) Sister told H back story "Philosophical line in their favour" "To kill a mockingbird"
+50 Sister "Where am I to find him?"
+51 Victoria Techno link to (Safe house)
+52 Int. (Contractor's Home) Unusual Killers being milked
+53 Sister (Safe House) H "With or without your help"
+54 Int. Unusual Killers with substance that kills. (Contractor's Home, descending)
+55 (Safe House) Techno gadgets A + H Sarcastic talk of old weapons.
+56 Victoria tells Sister to take out Big Boss but tracking him will uncover others.

**Tag:** A continuing storyline hinting about next week with a <u>brave</u> emotional Act Out.

+57 "Next Week" Sister (Target's Home) catches eye of Big Boss.

# L.A. SERIAL POOL

### *"Murder in the fourth"*

<u>Concurring scenes ready for shooting:</u>

#29 TAKES
#24 plot beats (A-12 B-8 C-4)

<u>KEY</u>

| | |
|---|---|
| ACT | Self explanatory. |
| **MINUTE** | **Page #** |
| **HERO'S JOURNEY ELEMENT** | **Essential stages #1-#7** |
| **CHARACTERS IN SCENE** | **Principals.** |
| **LOCATION** | **As is.** |

---

| | |
|---|---|
| PRE ACT I | Previously |
| MINUTE | 0-1 |
| HERO'S JOURNEY ELEMENT | (1)Establishing hero's world |
| CHARACTERS IN SCENE | ALEX HENRY |
| LOCATION | MONTAGE |

HENRY (V.O)
Previously on Serial Pool

| | |
|---|---|
| ACT | I |
| MINUTE | 1-4 |
| HERO'S JOURNEY ELEMENT | (1) Establishing hero's world |
| CHARACTERS IN SCENE | ALEX HENRY |
| LOCATION | EXT. STAKEOUT LOCATION #1 - DAY |

Voyeur ie: Car - ALEX and HENRY VICTORIA's personal life

| | |
|---|---|
| ACT | I |
| MINUTE | 4-6 |
| HERO'S JOURNEY ELEMENT | (2) Call to Adventure |
| CHARACTERS IN SCENE | ALEX HENRY |
| LOCATION | INT. SAFE HOUSE - DAY |

ALEX-HENRY Serial Killer's Home Trashed. Prowler.

| | |
|---|---|
| ACT | II |
| MINUTE | 18-20 |
| HERO'S JOURNEY ELEMENT | (3) Entering Mythological Woods |
| CHARACTERS IN SCENE | ALEX HENRY |
| LOCATION | INT. SAFE HOUSE - DAY |

| | |
|---|---|
| ACT | III |
| MINUTE | 37 |
| HERO'S JOURNEY ELEMENT | (4) Trail of Trials |
| CHARACTERS IN SCENE | ALEX HENRY |

# L.A. SERIAL POOL

## *"Murder in the fourth"*

| | |
|---|---|
| LOCATION | INT. SAFE HOUSE – DAY |

| | |
|---|---|
| ACT | IV |
| MINUTE | 54-57 |
| HERO'S JOURNEY ELEMENT | (7) Master of Both Worlds |
| CHARACTERS IN SCENE | ALEX HENRY |
| LOCATION | INT. SAFE HOUSE – DAY |

| | |
|---|---|
| ACT | II |
| MINUTE | 6-9 |
| HERO'S JOURNEY ELEMENT | (2) Call to Adventure |
| CHARACTERS IN SCENE | VICTORIA |
| LOCATION | EXT. MEETING PLACE – DAY |

VICTORIA THERAPIST OFFICE ie: Restaurant she stands him up.

| | |
|---|---|
| ACT | II |
| MINUTE | 15 |
| HERO'S JOURNEY ELEMENT | (2) Call to Adventure |
| CHARACTERS IN SCENE | VICTORIA |
| LOCATION | EXT. MEETING PLACE – DAY |

| | |
|---|---|
| ACT | II |
| MINUTE | 20-22 |
| HERO'S JOURNEY ELEMENT | (3) Enter mythological woods |
| CHARACTERS IN SCENE | VICTORIA |
| LOCATION | INT. TARGET'S HOME – DAY |

TARGET Warn of Contractor. Double crossed. The TARGET is the bad guy after all.

| | |
|---|---|
| ACT | III |
| MINUTE | 48-50 |
| HERO'S JOURNEY ELEMENT | (4) Trail of Trials |
| CHARACTERS IN SCENE | VICTORIA |
| LOCATION | INT. TARGET'S HOME – DAY |

| | |
|---|---|
| ACT | IV |
| MINUTE | 52-54 |
| HERO'S JOURNEY ELEMENT | |
| CHARACTERS IN SCENE | VICTORIA |
| LOCATION | INT. TARGET'S HOME – DAY |

| | |
|---|---|
| ACT | II |
| MINUTE | 22-23 |
| HERO'S JOURNEY ELEMENT | (2) Call to Adventure |
| CHARACTERS IN SCENE | VICTORIA |
| LOCATION | INT. TARGET'S HOME (DESCENT) – DAY |

# L.A. *serial pool*

# L.A. SERIAL POOL

## *"Murder in the fourth"*

```
ACT                          II
MINUTE                       16-18
HERO'S JOURNEY ELEMENT       (3) Entering Mythological Woods
CHARACTERS IN SCENE          VICTORIA
LOCATION                     INT. STAKEOUT LOCATION #2 - DAY
Voyeur ie: Plaza TARGET-Business life With Victoria


ACT                          II
MINUTE                       25-26
HERO'S JOURNEY ELEMENT       (4) Trail of Trials
CHARACTERS IN SCENE          VICTORIA
LOCATION                     INT. STAKEOUT LOCATION #3 - DAY
Voyeur ie: Hotel. Personal life With Victoria


ACT                          II
MINUTE                       27-28
HERO'S JOURNEY ELEMENT       (4) Trail of Trials
CHARACTERS IN SCENE          VICTORIA
LOCATION                     INT. STAKEOUT LOCATION #3 - DAY


ACT                          II
MINUTE                       23-25
HERO'S JOURNEY ELEMENT       (3) Entering Mythological Woods
CHARACTERS IN SCENE          VICTORIA
LOCATION                     INT. POLICE STATION - DAY


ACT                          III
MINUTE                       42-42
HERO'S JOURNEY ELEMENT       (4) Trail of Trials
CHARACTERS IN SCENE          VICTORIA
LOCATION                     INT. PLACE OF PERIL - NIGHT


ACT                          IV
MINUTE                       50-51
HERO'S JOURNEY ELEMENT       (5) Encounter the Evil one
CHARACTERS IN SCENE          VICTORIA
LOCATION                     INT. PLACE OF PERIL - NIGHT
- MULTIPLE FLASHBACKS


ACT                          II
MINUTE                       15-16
HERO'S JOURNEY ELEMENT       (3) Entering Mythological Woods
CHARACTERS IN SCENE          VICTORIA
LOCATION                     FLASHBACK
```

# L.A. SERIAL POOL

## *"Murder in the fourth"*

```
ACT                      III
MINUTE                   39-39
HERO'S JOURNEY ELEMENT   (4) Trail of Trials
CHARACTERS IN SCENE      VICTORIA
LOCATION                 FLASHBACK


ACT                      IV
MINUTE                   51
HERO'S JOURNEY ELEMENT   (5) Gaining the Hero's prize
CHARACTERS IN SCENE      VICTORIA
LOCATION                 FLASHBACK


ACT                      III
MINUTE                   35-36
HERO'S JOURNEY ELEMENT   (4) Trail of Trials
CHARACTERS IN SCENE      VICTORIA
LOCATION                 INT. CONTRACTOR'S HOME- DAY
Obstacle: Unable to see contractor.


ACT                      III
MINUTE                   42-42
HERO'S JOURNEY ELEMENT   (4) Trail of Trials
CHARACTERS IN SCENE      VICTORIA
LOCATION                 EXT/INT. CONTRACTOR'S HOME- DAY


ACT                      IV
MINUTE                   51-52
HERO'S JOURNEY ELEMENT   (5) Encountering the Evil One
CHARACTERS IN SCENE      VICTORIA
LOCATION                 INT. CONTRACTOR'S HOME - NIGHT


ACT                      IV
MINUTE                   52-52
HERO'S JOURNEY ELEMENT   (5) Encountering the Evil One
CHARACTERS IN SCENE      VICTORIA
LOCATION                 INT. CONTRACTOR'S (DESCENT) - NIGHT
```

# L.A. SERIAL POOL

## *"Murder in the fourth"*

`YELLOW CARDS`

```
ACT                        II
MINUTE                     14-15
HERO'S JOURNEY ELEMENT     (3) Entering mythological woods
CHARACTERS IN SCENE        VICTORIA
LOCATION                   EXT. VICTORIA'S OFFICE - DAY
 - TECH DEPT.
CONTRACTOR mission. Mission reminder.

ACT                        III
MINUTE                     32-35
HERO'S JOURNEY ELEMENT     (4) Trail of Trials
CHARACTERS IN SCENE        VICTORIA
LOCATION                   EXT. VICTORIA'S OFFICE - DAY
 -TECH DEPT.

ACT                        III
MINUTE                     36-37
HERO'S JOURNEY ELEMENT     (4) Trail of Trials
CHARACTERS IN SCENE        VICTORIA
LOCATION                   EXT. VICTORIA'S OFFICE - DAY

ACT                        III
MINUTE                     37-38
HERO'S JOURNEY ELEMENT     (4) Trail of Trials
CHARACTERS IN SCENE        VICTORIA
LOCATION                   EXT. VICTORIA'S OFFICE - DAY
 - TECH DEPT.

ACT                        III
MINUTE                     40-42
HERO'S JOURNEY ELEMENT     (4) Trail of Trials
CHARACTERS IN SCENE        VICTORIA
LOCATION                   EXT. VICTORIA'S OFFICE - DAY
```

# L.A. SERIAL POOL

## *"Murder in the fourth"*

EXT. STAKEOUT LOCATION #1 – DAY
(1) Establishing Heroes World eg: COORS FIELD

INT. SAFE HOUSE – DAY
(2) Call to Adventure

EXT. MEETING PLACE – DAY
(3) Entering the Mythological Woods eg: RECORD STORE

INT. STAKEOUT LOCATION #2 – DAY
(4) Trail of trials eg: MORGUE

INT. VICTORIA'S HOME - DAY
(4) Trail of trials INT. MALIBU COLONY

INT. TECH DEPT (VICTORIA'S OFFICE) - DAY
(4) Trail of trials INT. TECH DEPT, MALIBU COLONY

CHILDHOOD FLASHBACK INT. DOWNTOWN L.A.   THERAPIST OFFICE
Told from the Therapist's chair.

INT. ACTION LOCATION – NIGHT
(4) Trial (Obstacle resulting in Death) eg: Nightclub

INT. POLICE STATION – DAY
(4) Trail of trials (Obstruction)

EXT. STAKEOUT LOCATION #3 – DAY
(4) Trail of trials eg: ARCADE

INT. CONTRACTOR'S HOME – DAY
(4) Trail of trials (Stealthy/unseen) eg: APARTMENT

INT. PLACE OF PERIL – NIGHT
(4) Trial (Sense of foreboding) eg: Deserted building

INT. TARGET'S HOME – DAY
(5) Encounter the evil one.
INT. NEWPORT BEACH - LOVELL BEACH HOUSE

EXT. TARGET'S HOME (DESCENT) - DAY
(6) Gaining the Hero's prize Eg: FIRE ESCAPE
EXT. NEWPORT BEACH - LOVELL BEACH HOUSE

(7) Returning that prize to the community

# L.A. SERIAL POOL

## *"Murder in the fourth"*

Feature locations:
    EXT. SAN CLEMENTE - HILLY SUBURBAN GARDEN
    EXT. HUNTINGTON BEACH - END OF PIER (BEACH SHOP)
    INT. DOWNTOWN L.A. - PET SHOP
    INT. DOWNTOWN L.A. - THERAPIST OFFICE
    EXT. L.A. - PEACE AWARENESS LABYRINTH AND GARDENS
    INT. MEMORIAL PARK - ST.PETER'S EPISCOPAL CHURCH,
    INT. HOTEL ANAHEIM - SWIMMING POOL

TARGET'S HOME – BADDIE ABODE
    INT. NEWPORT BEACH - LOVELL BEACH HOUSE
        Body boarders - Surfer's walk of Fame.

INT. SAN DIEGO COUNTY - OCEANSIDE SAFE HOUSE
        Metrolink commuter train line connects Downtown LA with Orange
        County down to San Clamente, but continues on to Oceanside in San
        Diego County, from where you can pick up that region's Coaster and
        connect to downtown San Diego.

INT. MALIBU COLONY - TECH DEPT, VICTORIA'S OFFICE,

FAST-FOOD JOINT
FREE-SPIRITED BAR
UPSCALE RESTAURANT
DYNAMIC CLUB
THEME PARK – HOLLYWOOD STUDIOS – ART MUSEUM
SEEDY SUBURBS
HIGH-GLOSS NEIGHBORHOOD
QUIRKY SHOPPING STRIP MALLS
BOARDWALK
EXT. ORANGE GROVES

Eye-popping billboards, Painted Murals, All-night Delis, Neon signs, Palm tress.

Compact Neighborhoods:
    Venice
    Old Pasadena
        Car - Parking Lot – Public Transport
    Hollywood, Bars
    West Hollywood, Clubs
    West L.A.
    Santa Monica, Restaurants

Largest Port in the country. Transpacific trade. Financial hub.

Social: Racial divisions – 1992 riots. Mexican-American, Hispanic, Zimbabwe

# L.A. SERIAL POOL

## *"Murder in the fourth"*

Episode Titles & Subplots:

Feature title: L.A. Serial Pool (*Serial Pool Attendant*)

Series title: L.A. Serial Pool

Pilot Episode: *Murder in the fourth* (World Series)

- <u>(One-hour Format):</u> MURDER IN THE FOURTH

  ACT I
  o  Pre-emptive strike

  ACT II
  o  Bench the plan.

  ACT III
  o  Home Run

  ACT IV
  o  Queer eye for a bad guy

Episode II: *The Venice Cup* / MB Games (Europe)

  ACT I
  o  Deaf to your screams.

      SHOWCASE WORLD INNOVATIONS
              eg: Jet powered canoe.

Episode III: *Vacation - A Fisherman's Friend*
      ACT I
      o  The Jump.

Subplot: To catch a Slasher.

--------------------------

"L.A. Serial Pool, The Feature, Series-Bible and Pilot-Episode are under revision.
There have been developmental amendments since last publication. Contributions
welcome"

                    "Take me home. Give me some loving.
        To the prosperous future of L.A. Serial Pool."
                                        Karl Peter Smith

## SPECIAL ACKNOWLEDGEMENTS

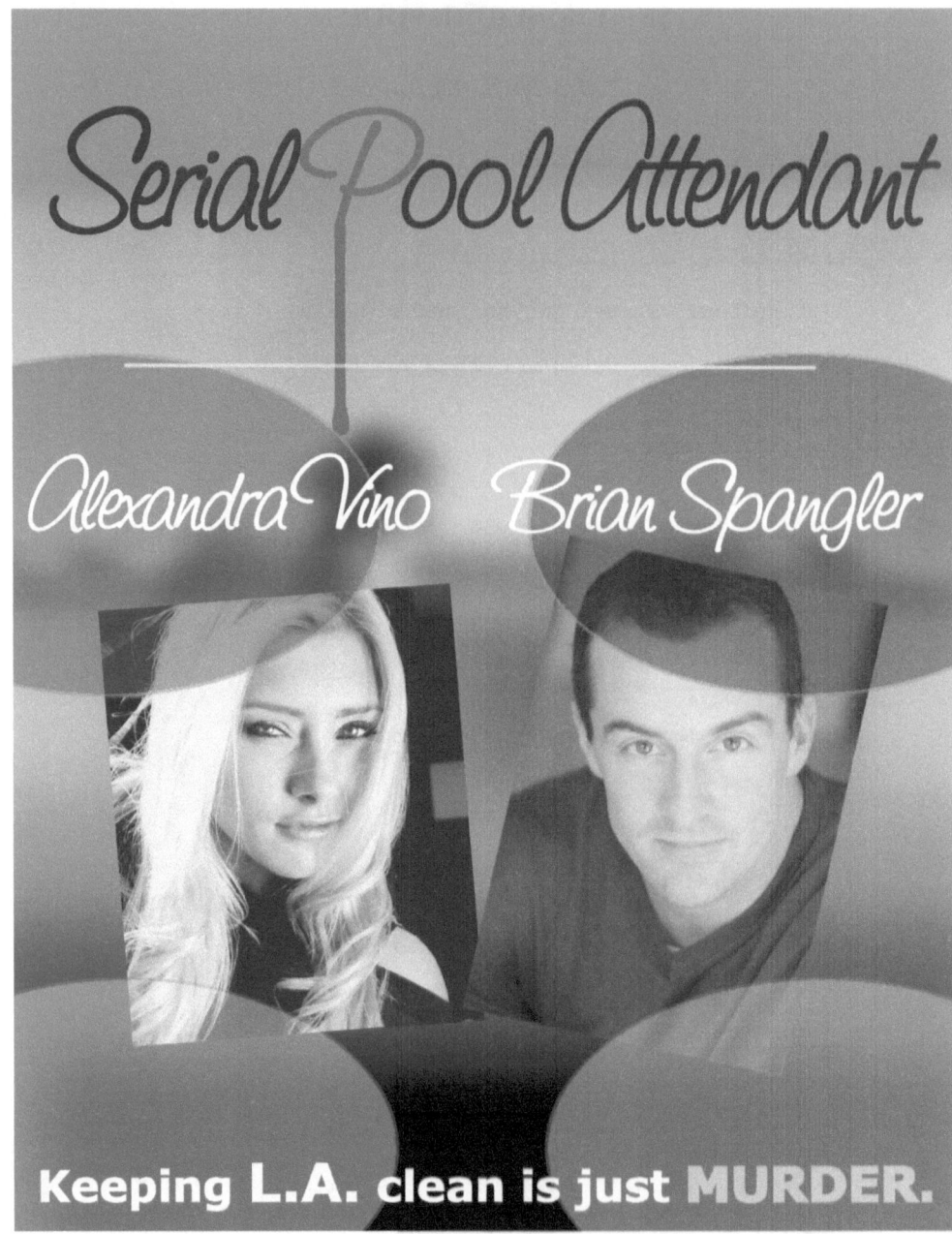

*Serial Pool Attendant*

*Alexandra Vino*     *Brian Spangler*

Keeping **L.A.** clean is just **MURDER.**

(BOTH HAVE GREEN EYES)

ACTORS attached as interested parties.

*'Moving words around a page is like painting.'*
To learn this process check out... Print-on-demand Technical Guide: Screenplay Publishing

*Karl Peter Smith*

Pencil Drawing of Miss. Helen Shepley by K.S. 2006

### E-PORTFOLIO:
1. Search for Eurydice - Romance with Bite
2. Serial Pool Attendant - Crime
3. Naked Spurs - Western
4. A History of Fear - Horror
5. Purge the Soul – Thriller
6. Memoirs of Dirty Max - Romance
7. Bikini THREE-20 (Thunderbirds) – Sci-Fi
8. Bill and Ted's Idiot's Guide to Screenwriting - Comedy

### EDUCATION
UNIVERSITY OF TEESSIDE, Cleveland, England.
Bachelor of Fine Art - Printing, Drawing and Painting.
Specialized in Sculpture

### HONOURS
Cleveland College of Art and Design used my sculptures to advertise the college in the UCAS prospectus; a national publication attracting future students to campus.

*"I cried whilst writing."*
## A History Of Fear
*"...the blonde ponytail."*

*Thanks Helen x*

**"If you completely storyboard a movie you neuter possibilities for happy accidents"**
**- Gore Verbinski, *Director of Pirates of the Caribbean: Curse of the Black Pearl.***

A story that will appeal to general readers and classicists alike.

When the reputations of two gods hinge on the actions of one man expect all hell to break loose when gun-toting Argonauts descend all-guns-blazing to the Underworld.

Orpheus's wife is not quite dead yet!

*He must find her.*

"Clutching my sister, heavy, dead in my arms; my cries for help drowned out by the music of the Pool hall. One Greek hero had been here before me; Orpheus."
- Karl Peter Smith, *The Author.*

email: orphichouse@yahoo.co.uk          titles available from all good book stores

Greek mythology

Comic book, scripts

Graphic Novels

FICTION

SEARCH FOR EURYDICE:
SCREENPLAY AND GRAPHIC NOVEL

**HARDBACK**
**ISBN 978-0-9566156-6-4**

**PAPERBACK**
**ISBN 978-0-9566156-0-2**

BOOK SIZE: US LETTER 8"x11.5"

KARL SMITH

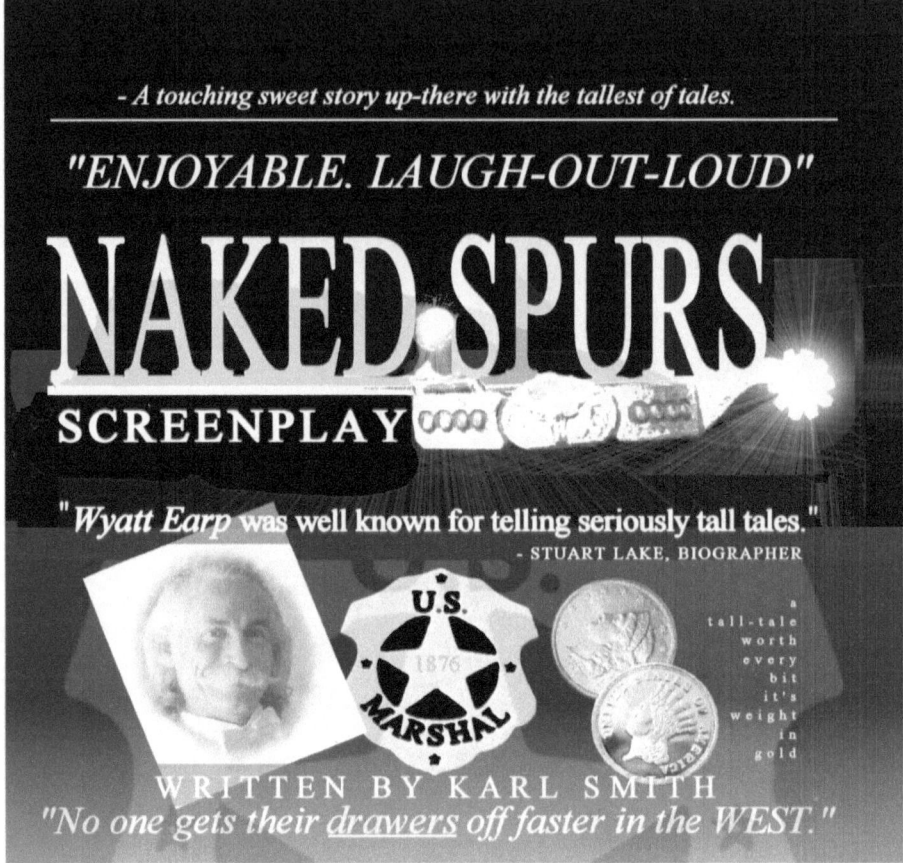

*- A touching sweet story up-there with the tallest of tales.*

## "ENJOYABLE. LAUGH-OUT-LOUD"

# NAKED SPURS

## SCREENPLAY

"*Wyatt Earp* was well known for telling seriously tall tales."
- STUART LAKE, BIOGRAPHER

a
tall-tale
worth
every
bit
it's
weight
in
gold

WRITTEN BY KARL SMITH

"*No one gets their <u>drawers</u> off faster in the WEST.*"

"*Naked but for a pair of spurs*"

"*Did one man truely outwit the greatest gunslingers in history?*"

"*I do sincerely wish it were true.*"

- California 1876 -

# NAKED SPURS

"NO ONE GETS THEIR DRAWERS OFF FASTER IN THE WEST"

## CALIFORNIA 1876

### A COAST MIWOK WARRIOR
### AND THE PRISON THAT WAS TO BE NAMED AFTER HIM

*Saint ...*     *... Quentin*

**A YOUNG ARTIST** creates a Wild West diorama and tells the seriously tall tale of NAKED SPURS, his great-great grandfather.

**NAKED SPURS** is the plausible tale of the BEAT THE BOUNTY competition a contest attracting the fastest guns in the West to the largest manhunt in history.

As the streaking inmate of San Quentin penitentiary **NAKED SPURS** must run for his life along with other criminals.

This is one story he cannot run away from.

**"FROM THE MAN WITH BALLS IS BORN A LEGEND."**

Inspiration:

Wyatt Earp told his memoirs to his biographer Stuart Lake.
In one story he was suspected of fixing a prize fight in which he was the judge.
The book was suspected to be entirely fictional.

Concept:

*'The Good, the Bad and the Ugly'* meets *'My name is Earl'* ... well, Earp actually.

**About the Author**
Karl Smith graduated with a degree in Fine Art from Cleveland College of Art and Design. His fresh fusion of action and emotion when screenwriting is surely to be seen in a cinema near you soon. Bet your mortgage on it!

**HARDBACK**
THE SOUND OF NAKED SPURS:
A SPAGHETTI WESTERN SCREENPLAY
ISBN 978-0-9566156-8-8

**PAPERBACK**
NAKED SPURS: SCREENPLAY
ISBN 978-0-9566156-2-6

*Karl Peter Smith*

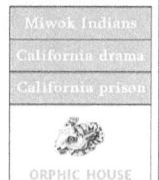

Miwok Indians
California drama
California prison

ORPHIC HOUSE

# A HISTORY OF FEAR

### SCREENPLAY

## SCREENPLAY
### WRITTEN BY
*karl smith*

*"Will put the frighteners up you."*
*"A GRIPPING TALE!"*

# A HISTORY OF FEAR

Synopsis:
A wish melds the soul of a kind-hearted simpleton to a toy BEAR. A secret for three generations, the seven foot GUARDIAN wakes in time of need.

Surviving the sinking of the TITANIC a toy BEAR passes into the hands of the JEWISH COMMUNITY. Aboard the rescue ship CARPATHIA it travels on to the gas chambers of AUSCHWITZ.

The BEAR brings something with it…A HISTORY OF FEAR.

When TRICK OR TREATERS uncover an SS OFFICER in the neighborhood . . .

## *HALLOWEEN IS ABOUT TO GET A LITTLE HAIRY*

Concept:
'Gremlins' meets 'Schindler's List' / 'The Golem of Prague'.

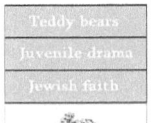

Teddy bears
Juvenile drama
Jewish faith

ORPHIC HOUSE

A HISTORY OF FEAR:
SCREENPLAY

**HARDBACK**
ISBN 978-0-9566156-9-5

**PAPERBACK**
ISBN 978-0-9566156-3-3

KARL SMITH